# Freedom was the only thing on her mind

Hannah pressed herself against the locked door. He must have read the fear in her eyes, because he said gently, ''I'm not going to hurt you. And unless there's a rapid change in the weather, we're going to be holed up here for some time. It would be easier for both of us if you'd stop looking like a frightened rabbit.''

''How do you expect me to look?'' she snapped.
''Happy? I get kidnapped by some lunatic, get hauled halfway across England in a blizzard and dumped in a shack.''

''With good reason, Hannah. I know everything about you,'' he said. ''Now, give me your coat and take off those wet boots.''

''No.'' Hannah was shaking inside as well as out as he advanced toward her, tall, powerful, menacing—and entirely much too male.

**Diana Hamilton** creates high-tension conflict
that brings new life to traditional romance.
Readers find her a welcome addition to the
Harlequin Romance line and will be glad to know
that more novels by this talented author are
already in the works.

## Books by Diana Hamilton

HARLEQUIN ROMANCE
2865—IMPULSIVE ATTRACTION
2959—PAINTED LADY

HARLEQUIN PRESENTS
993—SONG IN A STRANGE LAND

Don't miss any of our special offers. Write to us at the
following address for information on our newest releases.

Harlequin Reader Service
901 Fuhrmann Blvd., P.O. Box 1397, Buffalo, NY 14240
Canadian address: P.O. Box 603,
Fort Erie, Ont. L2A 5X3

# THE WILD SIDE
# Diana Hamilton

## *Harlequin Books*

TORONTO • NEW YORK • LONDON
AMSTERDAM • PARIS • SYDNEY • HAMBURG
STOCKHOLM • ATHENS • TOKYO • MILAN

Original hardcover edition published in 1988
by Mills & Boon Limited

ISBN 0-373-02979-9

Harlequin Romance first edition May 1989

# CHAPTER ONE

'THREE weeks isn't a lifetime, Gerald.'

Gerald Orme had been saying he'd miss her and now he told Hannah sulkily, 'It might as well be. You know how I feel about you. I could have come with you, but you wouldn't have it.'

'It wouldn't have been a good idea.' Hannah's generous mouth firmed as her slender fingers twisted the stem of the wine glass on the olive linen table covering. The Bollinger was excellent; Gerald had turned what he'd said would be a simple dinner for two into something that reeked of elegance and style. He was obviously planning ahead, optimistically looking beyond the 'goodnight and thank you and see you in three weeks' that she was planning to use to terminate the evening on her doorstep.

But the whole point of her agreeing to have dinner with him tonight had been to tell him, for definitely the last time, that sorry, but she could never feel anything for him beyond friendliness as an individual and respect as a colleague.

She had accepted dates with him occasionally simply because it had been less wearing than repeatedly turning his invitations down, but she had never once given him grounds to hope that anything more than friendship could ever grow between them. And now, because she would be away from the agency for three weeks, he had decided to make another attempt to get her to see things his way.

'I hate to think of you lying on sun-soaked beaches alone, prey to every passing wolf.' The expression in his light brown eyes echoed the now belligerent jut of his chin.

Hannah said crisply, 'Marrakesh isn't on the coast, as you know very well, and I shall spend a lot of my time up on the Atlas ski-slopes, so if anyone picks me up it will be because I've fallen flat on my face.'

'Whatever...' Gerald put in waspishly, not in the mood for humour. 'I still don't see why we couldn't have gone together. Father and Joyce could have held the fort. I want you with me all the time. I want to marry you.'

'Gerald—please——' Suddenly, Hannah was desperate to get home. The evening had been a disaster; she should never have given way to his insistent yet lightly teasing plea that she have dinner with him. 'Nothing special—mainly so that we can chew over the state of the art in peace—any problems or queries that might come up while you're away. I won't come on heavy, I promise!'

Yet he had done nothing but, and work hadn't been mentioned. Not that she could see any problems on that score; she'd tied up loose ends. She was efficient and loved her work. The Orme Literary Agency was successful in the firm hands of Roger Orme, Gerald's father, and during the time she'd been with him she had, so he said, become his 'right-hand man'. But Gerald was starting to irritate her, which was a pity because when he forgot his ridiculous infatuation he could be a charming companion, a reliable colleague. He was twenty-four years old but at times like these, Hannah, at twenty-five, felt a hundred years his senior.

Her startlingly vivid green eyes were clouded with aggravation as she strove to find the right words. She had to get it through his head, once and for all, that she wasn't interested in him in that way. But she couldn't be too withering. She had to work with him. Besides, she didn't like hurting anyone.

Turning her head so that the kicked-spaniel look in his eyes wouldn't soften her, make her say something he might construe as hope, her eyes swept around the discreetly elegant restaurant to be drawn almost immediately and irrevocably, it seemed, to those of the man who sat alone at the adjoining table. For a timeless moment their eyes held, then thick dark lashes lowered as Hannah's slid away, quick hot colour flooding the pallor of her creamy skin.

She was accustomed to masculine stares—admiring, speculative or frankly lustful—stares that roved over the delicate oval of her face, the upswept heavy dark hair, the supple grace of her body. She had grown so accustomed that she now had no difficulty ignoring them. But this man was impossible to ignore. He was handsome, almost severely so. Dark, with the brooding quality that subtly hinted at danger. And when her eyes had met his she had felt sucked into those cold dark depths and had known, distinctly and instinctively, that he had been watching her for quite some time, that she was no stranger to him. It was a disconcerting thought.

He was dining alone, and the only fault one could find with Antoine's was the proximity of the tables. Half turning in her seat, Hannah presented him coolly with the long, graceful line of an excluding shoulder, the smooth sheen of satin skin, exposed by the halter neckline of her tawny-red silk jersey dress, already, annoyingly, prickling as she felt the searing touch of his cold black eyes.

He couldn't help but have overheard their conversation, perhaps been amused by what he might have translated as a lovers' tiff. Yet there had been no amusement in the eyes that had held hers, only a chilling disdain.

Thrusting the stranger and the odd effect he had had on her out of her mind, she smiled tiredly at Gerald.

'I'd like to go home now.' And she watched as, red faced, he beckoned for the bill.

Hannah prowled around her mews flat, restlessness implicit in every line of her tall, graceful body as her eyes swept unseeingly over the muted décor of misty greens and greys, the bits and pieces of antique furniture she had collected during her time there, the old rosewood and mahogany blending successfully with the peacock-blue-upholstered cane loungers.

Since Gerald had left an hour ago she had done her last-minute packing, phoned the cab operators to make sure they had the right time for the morning—five-thirty on the dot—and had heated herself a cup of milk. But she still couldn't face the idea of bed, felt too edgy, as if something, someone, were lying in wait around the corner, a feeling which she knew to be totally absurd.

Inviting Gerald in after their dinner date had been about the last thing she'd had in mind. But what she'd had to say to him would have been impossible in the restaurant, as it had turned out, with the cold-eyed stranger listening to every word.

Gerald had tried to take her in his arms the moment the flat door was closed, but she had evaded him, going to make coffee, telling him as he followed her through to the kitchen like a hopeful puppy,

'I offered you coffee so that we could talk in peace. Just talk, Gerald. I have to make you understand that there can never be anything between us—except friendship, of course, and a good working relationship. Anything else is out.'

'I want to marry you,' he had said, as if that made a difference, his mood suddenly truculent, and Hannah had put the mugs and cream on the tray, biting her lips, striving to hold on to the patience that was rapidly leaving her.

'Marriage is out.'

'What have you got against it?' He had followed as she carried the tray through to the sitting-room, leaning against the door frame, watching as she put the tray on the hearth and flicked on the electric fire to boost the central heating, an attempt to evict the chill that was due more to something inside her than the ambient temperature in the flat.

'Nothing. For the right people.'

'Are you frigid? Gay?' He had closed the door with a vicious bang and she had said, 'Neither,' pouring the coffee, her face turned so that he shouldn't see her sudden pallor, the way her hands shook...

Twice she had been on the brink of marriage, although the first time, when she had been nineteen, it had only been in her mind, certainly not in Edward's. And that was her own business, not Gerald's. But her engagement to Eden had been fairly common knowledge and if she told him what had happened he might understand why romantic involvements were not for her.

'I was engaged, not so long ago,' she told Gerald, handing him his coffee. 'To Eden Wilmott. The way things turned out, it put me off marriage for life.'

'Wilmott?' he echoed, frowning as if reaching for something just beyond memory. 'Joyce mentioned something—didn't he have a runaway bestseller?'

'That's right. His first book. Your father handled that for him—I took over while he was trying to write his second.' She took her own mug, pacing the floor, remembering how difficult Eden had found the work, how she had tried to help, how Eden had seemed dependent on her. He had needed her, and for Hannah, who had a generous nature, that had felt good.

'So what happened?' Gerald wanted to know, sprawled out on one of the loungers, his mouth sulky.

Hannah shrugged. 'The usual.' Only there hadn't been anything usual or ordinary about it. Her growing relationship with Eden had made her feel safe to begin with. So safe. Her feelings for him hadn't touched the heights she had ascended to during her brief and fraught relationship with Edward Sage, but it hadn't touched the killing depths, either.

Her mouth twisted wryly as she recalled how Lottie, Eden's mother, had told her how Eden needed marriage. A caring partner, unlike Donald, their other, older son. 'Donald would never settle,' Lottie had said, 'but I came to terms with that long ago. It doesn't worry me— Donald's self-sufficient, a little on the wild side—always has been.' And Hannah had had the distinct impression that although his parents were immensely proud of Donald, perhaps a little in awe of him, it was Eden who was so plainly adored.

Hannah had asked, 'Where is Donald? Shall I get to meet him?' and Eden, surly for the first time with her, had turned away, shrugging. 'In Hong Kong. On business. And I'm not sure enough of you to want you to meet him, so he can stay there forever as far as I'm concerned. He has the devil's own way with women.'

The same type as Edward, Hannah had decided, dismissing him. She had had enough of macho, womanising charm to last her a lifetime. She felt safe with Eden. Safe enough to believe that marriage to him could echo the quiet perfection of her parents' marriage. They were both dead now, that devoted, loving couple, and Hannah still missed the undemanding love that had always been there, waiting for her in the peaceful country vicarage.

'And what the hell does "the usual" mean?' Gerald's peevish tones broke her reverie, reminding her of his existence. She leant against a rosewood chiffonier, her eyes startled, skirting round the truth—the truth that had shocked her to the core when it had been presented to her a couple of months before they were to have been married.

'He had problems,' she told him stiffly, editing carefully. 'I tried every way I knew to help him, but the more I tried, the more he resented it. In the end I had to break the engagement off. It taught me never to put my happiness in any man's hands.'

'Gave you a full-blown phobia, you mean. Well, phobias can be cured.' He got to his feet and his voice was dry. 'This must have all happened while I was in the States, before I came back to join Dad at the agency. Am I to take it that he took himself off our list? Found another agent? Did you lose us our slice of his sky-high earnings?'

'No.' Hannah's emerald eyes were bleak. 'He died in a car accident on the night before we were to have been married.' She had been fighting guilt over that ever since she had known that he had been senseless-drunk while driving on that fatal night. It surely hadn't been her fault? What more could she have done? She had tried everything she knew to help him.

And she didn't feel guilty, she told herself desperately as she watched Gerald walk out of the flat. Saddened, yes—particularly for his parents...for that wasted talent. But not guilty. Surely, not guilty!

Hannah had set the alarm for four-thirty but woke before it went off. Rolling out of bed, stripping it, she carried the sheets to the bathroom and stuffed them in the linen basket, washed and dressed in a burgundy-coloured fine wool and silk jumpsuit—comfortable for travelling in— and plaited her heavy soft hair in a single thick dark braid. A minimum of make-up and she was ready for breakfast—milk and an apple. As her even white teeth sank into the crisp fruit she mentally went through her check list. She didn't think she'd forgotten anything and the only thing left to do was turn off the water and the central heating.

A little before five-thirty she caught the sound of a car crawling down the silent street outside, followed, a few moments later, by a double ring on her doorbell.

The cab already. She glanced at her watch. Ten minutes too early. But no matter. She opened the door where her suitcase was waiting and the driver said, 'Miss Sloane for Gatwick?' his face in shadow as he bent to pick up the luggage, his voice cool, impersonal.

'Thank you.' She turned back into the flat for a brief check that her passport, tickets, travellers' cheques were all present and correct before shrugging into her waist-length fur jacket and swinging the strap of her flight bag over her shoulder.

She was now beginning to look forward to this holiday, beginning to see it more as a time for relaxing, for enjoyment, than a much-needed break from Gerald's pursuance and the awkwardness it could cause between herself and her boss. Roger Orme respected her as an employee, for her ability to pick winners from the mass of mediocrity that arrived unsolicited in every post, and for her innate tact when dealing with the more difficult of their clients. It was an art, she guessed, that she had picked up from helping her father around his parish when she had been in her teens.

Yes, Roger Orme liked her as a person, but he loved his son. And if he thought she was making Gerald unhappy, even though she had given him no encouragement, then things could get tricky and she might find herself having to resign from a well-paid job, one which she enjoyed. So this holiday would give both herself and Gerald a much-needed breathing space—and she would enjoy it. Already she could feel the beginnings of anticipation tingle through her bones.

The area in front of the mews cottages was dark, illuminated only by a single lamp. It was raining heavily, flakes of snow in the rain, and Hannah drew the deep collar on her coat up, the dark sable softness cosseting her face. She turned to the street to where the car was parked in the shadows between the twin pools of light from the street lamp that glistened amber on the wet pavements.

The driver straightened after stowing her luggage in the boot, looking big and burly in his rain-dampened sheepskin, the light from the lamps not touching his face. Impatiently, she felt, as if he thought they were late and not early, he opened the rear door of the sleek car, nodding curtly as she slipped gratefully into the cocooning warmth of the interior, hurrying to get out of the sleet, not looking at him, her thoughts pleasant, light.

He didn't seem in the mood to talk, his surly attitude probably due to having to leave the warmth and comfort of his bed at such an hour, on such a morning. Consigning him to his bad mood, she closed her eyes, listening to the muted purr of the engine, the hiss of tyres on the wet road.

This would be the first real holiday she'd taken since going to work for Roger Orme. She had felt too shattered by the deaths of her parents; she had always spent her breaks at home with them in their country vicarage. And then there had been Eden, and after she had broken with him she had decided to move. With the modest but comfortable legacy from her parents she had moved from her bed-sit to the mews flat and had furnished and decorated it with the care and style she was learning to extend to her own appearance—the clothes she wore, the perfume and cosmetics she used.

There was little traffic on the roads at this time of the morning, and the driver was putting his foot down, intent on burning the miles, so she should be at Gatwick with time to spare for a coffee, a browse around the bookshop.

It had been late before she had got to bed last night and then she had slept only fitfully, so now her eyelids drooped as she relaxed in the comfort of the leather-upholstered rear seat, the view from the window at her side a blur of street lights in the wet darkness.

It was growing a little lighter when she woke, the car still moving relentlessly on, and Hannah, disorientated, saw a road sign for Ipswich, briefly illuminated in the glare of the headlamps, before falling away behind them. Twisting in her seat, she stared illogically after the rapidly

retreating sign, as if that could help her to make sense
out of what was going on.

Jerking round again, she tried to read the time, but
the interior of the car was still too dark for her to be
able to see the digits on her wristwatch.

'Driver——' She leaned forward, touching his
shoulder. 'We should be at Gatwick by now, and I'm
sure I saw a sign for Ipswich.'

She confidently expected a reassurance, something she
could laugh about later and tell her friends. 'I was half
asleep, thought he must have taken a wrong turn about
a hundred miles back!' She certainly hadn't expected
total silence, his complete dismissal of her words, the
touch of her hand on his shoulder, total and unnerving.

And a glance at his face for the first time, a hard look
at his profile in the dim light of the dashboard, was
enough to turn her cold, to constrict her breathing until
her heart pumped erratically.

Blank, unyielding, it told her nothing except that he
was the man who had looked at her so strangely, had
held her eyes with his for a timeless moment in the restaurant the night before.

Fully awake now, jerked savagely back to her senses,
she found a haughty tone, used it. 'I'm going to miss
my flight, and I'll make sure your company get to hear
of this.'

He ignored the threat, as he had ignored her before,
and she had the feeling that he would take as much notice
of anything she said or did as he would of the muted
buzzing of an expiring gnat. There was something
chilling, terrifying, about the deadly stillness inside the
car, the only sound the low growl of the engine, the remorseless hiss of the tyres on wet tarmac—carrying her
where?

His total lack of response had a nightmare quality, but then he spoke and she wished he hadn't because what he told her turned her sick, his words conveying a coldness that had nothing to do with the grey light of dawn, the driving snowflakes borne on gusts of the cold east wind.

# CHAPTER TWO

'FORGET your flight. I've something else in mind for you.'

'What the hell do you mean? I——' Hannah's words were cut off in her parched throat as he cut in brusquely, changing gear, his eyes on the road.

'And don't waste time trying to get out. The doors are locked.'

There was nothing she could say to that—to anything. The power of speech seemed to have deserted her and she felt mindless, bodyless almost, perched on the rear seat staring at the rhythmic movements of the wipers as they pushed the falling snow to little heaps at the sides of the windscreen where they thickened, grew, before sliding away into oblivion. Only the heavy thundering of her heart told her she was still functioning as a human being.

This was crazy. She didn't know this man, couldn't conceive why he should have decided to abduct her. Yet, sickeningly, she recalled the way those hard black eyes had seared her last night, as if he could shred her to little pieces with a look. She had had the instinctive feeling that she was no stranger to him, that he knew her inside out.

'What do you hope to gain from this?' Her voice, when it finally came, was a thin impoverished thread of sound, disembodied, not seeming to have anything to do with her, her mind an alien thing, its tormented thoughts totally foreign to her, to her way of life, to

what she knew of herself. *Kidnap?* Absurd! She didn't
have wealthy parents, a wealthy lover who would pay
big money for her safe return.

'If—if it's money——' Again the thin tortured voice
that seemed to have no part of her '—you've got the
wrong woman. There's no one to pay a ransom.'

The snow was falling as if it meant it now, the roads
empty except for a small van approaching, a muddy
green colour against the whiteness of the road, crawling.
Hannah beat small gloved fists against the window at
her side, yelling, frantically trying to alert the driver of
the van.

She glimpsed the woman's face as the two vehicles
came abreast; it was grimly intent on the treacherous
surface of the road ahead of her, Hannah's wild ges-
ticulations unnoticed, her shouts unheard. It made her
feel as though she were no longer living, had no
substance, and she could have wept with frustration, in
despair. She scrambled round in the seat, only to be
thrown off balance, jolting her head against the back of
the driver's seat as brakes were slammed on, the car
slowing to a halt.

She was still half on the floor, half on the seat, when
the door was flung open and he stood there, his mouth
a grimly determined line, cold air spiked with snow
gusting in.

'Get out.'

Fear-drowned eyes winged upwards, met the cold black
chips of ice that regarded her with hard intensity, wavered
and fell again. Hannah took a grip on herself. Physically, she was no match for him, but she wouldn't give
in without a fight. She had a brain and it was time she
started to use it.

He wasn't about to offer her her freedom, that would be the last thing on his mind, so she had to take it. Levering herself up on to the seat, her movements clumsy in the confined space, she slid carefully over it towards the open door where he stood, waiting for her with barely controlled impatience expressed in every line of the tall, commanding figure.

Muscles tensed in readiness for the last-minute surge of energy she must release like a spring if she were to outwit him, evade him, run like the wind and make the bid for freedom that could well be a matter of life or death, Hannah tried to make her movements seem sluggish, reluctant.

But he could either read her mind or he had a brain like a laser, one jump ahead, because as she told herself *Now! Go!* a strong hand snapped out and gripped her left arm and there was no throwing off that band of steel.

'You go where I take you. Stay where I put you. And if you've ideas of your own, forget them.' The icy severity in the tone, the utter dominance, touched a spot deep inside her and made her want to vomit, and the frustrated run of adrenalin in her burst out in a desperate, unthinking flailing of fists against the broad wall of his chest, booted feet flying, making contact with his cord-covered shins.

'Cool it, lady.' One effortless twist of the hand that held her hoisted her out of reach, held her as she squirmed impotently in his grasp, praying for the blessed sound of an approaching car.

Perhaps her anguished, silent prayer transmitted itself to him, or perhaps he'd been aware of the chance of a passing car and had taken it, because the risk was worth it, for he motioned her into the front of the car and, when she dug her heels in, refusing to budge, strong hands thrust her forward, sending her scrambling over the driver's seat.

'Sit where I can keep an eye on you. No more tricks.'

Red with rage and the humiliation of being shoved around like a sack of potatoes, Hannah forgot her fear of him for long enough to snap,

'Are you always so brutal? Is that the way you get your kicks?' And then the fear came back as her brilliantly angry green eyes met the cold black assessment of his, and she turned her head, her colour draining away as he re-started the engine, telling her,

'Fasten your seat-belt. And I don't use force unless I have to. Harming you is the last thing on my mind.'

His voice was low, deep, with a smoky quality that sent shivers over her skin. A cool trickle of fear feathered down her spine, making her shudder. Hannah stared at the twisting ribbon of road ahead, the snowflakes swirling from a leaden sky. Her mouth felt stiff, her lips wooden, but she forced the words past them, knowing there was nothing she could do to make him tell her anything he didn't choose to.

'Then what is on your mind? There's no one to pay to get me back.'

'I'm not aiming to gain financially from this. It's as distasteful to me as it is to you. You'll be free to go as soon as I've finished with you.'

Quickly, unbelievingly, she glanced at his profile. Severely handsome, concentrating on his driving in ever worsening weather conditions, it gave nothing away. If he didn't mean to harm her or hold her to ransom, then what? Rape?

Her heart kicked with sudden terror and she stared down at her hands, twisting frantically together in her lap. But common sense took over, and she was relieved she was still capable of logical thought. If rape had been on his mind he would have had the ideal opportunity when she'd opened the door to him earlier on.

The situation was growing more nightmarishly absurd by the moment. Why should a cab driver just make off with one of his passengers?

Except that he was no cab driver, of course!

Last night, over dinner, she'd given Gerald details—details which this man had overheard. The cab would be picking her up at five-thirty, she'd said, refusing his offer of a lift to Gatwick. And this man had tucked the information away in his mind, arrived early enough to give him a margin of safety before the real driver arrived, had said 'Miss Sloane for Gatwick?' and that had been that. But why?

They had by-passed Ipswich some time ago, were keeping to secondary roads—because of her earlier, abortive attempt to attract attention? she wondered. And at the top of a long steep incline which they barely made, she heard the low impatient suck of his indrawn breath before he veered left, taking a narrow snow-piled lane that looked as if it led nowhere.

The shrouded countryside was empty; stark skeletal trees, snow-burdened hedges and, once, the glimpse of a distant spire. They might be the only people left in the world, she thought, shuddering.

'Where the hell do you think you're taking me?' Her voice was tight with anger and fear. She hoped they got stranded, because wherever he was taking her was where she didn't care to be.

'Right now, to the cottage. I'd an entirely different location in mind.'

Which told her exactly nothing, she noted edgily. By now her flight would be on its way to Morocco, and she wasn't on it. No one would miss her for at least three weeks and the thought terrified her. If only she knew what was going on in his twisted mind.

'What's your name?' She might as well humour him, try to establish some kind of rapport. Aggression from her was a non-starter, there was no mileage in it, and she was considerably startled when he answered immediately, if in a hard voice,

'Waldo Ross.'

'Waldo,' she mused, deliberately playing a part. 'That's unusual.' And that elicited no response; it probably wasn't his real name. He'd be a fool if he revealed his true identity, and he certainly wasn't that.

There were times when she thought they wouldn't make it to the cottage, wherever that was, times when the lane grew narrower, the snow deeper, blown into drifts, but he drove well, she had to give him that, handling the car as if it were a living thing.

And then through a break in the drifting clouds of falling snow she saw the cottage. It had to be the one he was making for, like an animal to its lair; there was no other dwelling in sight. It was at the far side of what appeared to be a sea of unending whiteness, dark stone walls supporting a snow-laden roof. Small, no sign of life.

Her heart plummeted as he slid the car to a halt—'We walk from here. There's a damned great drift across the track.'—because perversely, she didn't want to leave the relative safety of the car now.

She had been frightened—terrified and confused was nearer the mark—but at least he hadn't touched her, or only to haul her out of the back and into the seat beside him. And that hadn't been because he'd wanted her close. He'd just wanted to make sure she didn't try to attract someone's attention again. But out there, in that wild winter wasteland, anything could happen.

The going was tough, although the man who said his name was Waldo Ross carried her case, and the free hand that gripped her arm, helping her as they floundered through the knee-high drifts, was surprisingly gentle. The surprising thought flickered through her head that if he were at her side, as a friend, she would never lack that gentle yet firm support. But she knew that if she made the slightest attempt to pull away, to run for it, that hand would tighten like an iron trap.

No smoke came from the single squat chimney and the front door was locked, and when he reached in an inside pocket for the key she wondered if this was the time to make a run for it. But even as the thought presented itself to her panicky brain, he said, precisely, coldly, 'Don't try it. You wouldn't get two yards.' So he was capable of reading her mind. The knowledge chilled her, kept her acquiescent as he opened the door and steered her inside, dropping her case on the floor of what had to be the living-room. There was no hallway, just a square, low-ceilinged room, comfortably furnished, cold, with a wide stone hearth where no fire burned.

Hannah pressed herself back against the closed and locked door as if to get that little bit closer to freedom and safety, and he must have read the fear in her deep green eyes because he said, in a softer tone than any she'd heard from him so far, 'I'm not going to hurt you. And unless there's a very rapid thaw we're going to be holed up together for some considerable time. So it would be easier for both of us if you stopped looking like a frightened rabbit.'

It was all that was needed to spark her fighting spirit back to life and she sucked in her breath, angry colour staining slanting cheekbones.

'How do you expect me to look? *Happy?* I get kidnapped by some lunatic who just happened to overhear that I was expecting a cab at five-thirty this morning, hauled half-way across the country in a blizzard, dumped in a shack. You tell me you won't hurt me, that you don't intend holding me to ransom. So what's wrong with you, anyway? Can't you think of anything better to do with your spare time?'

If she had believed him to be anything other than a raving lunatic she might have thought the upward twist of his hard male mouth, the sudden slight crinkle of lines at the corners of his hard black eyes, to be amusement, respect. But his next words drove everything else out of her mind.

'Nothing happened by accident. I know all I need or want to know about you, Hannah Sloane. I knew precisely when you'd be away from the agency, the time of your flight, the time you were being picked up, and where you lived. It was sheer coincidence that I sat near you and your latest besotted, bamboozled lover last night.'

That kept her quiet while he went to the hearth, taking kindling and firelighters from a copper coal scuttle, logs from a huge antique cast-iron missionary pot that stood on the stone hearth slabs. It gave her more to think about and it was, if possible, even more terrifying. To have found out her name, where she worked, the dates of her holiday, her flight, the time she'd booked the cab for, meant that he must have been keeping tabs on her for quite some time.

The idea of him prying into her private life was obscene, worse than the way he'd abducted her. It increased her vulnerability. This had not been a spur-of-the-moment act, committed by a crazy man, but a coldly calculated plan of campaign, every aspect dovetailing.

But he couldn't have taken the blizzard into consideration. It hadn't been forecast. Therefore, his plans, no matter how carefully formulated, were flawed. There had to be an opportunity there, somewhere.

He had the beginnings of a fire, flames licking the kindling, glowing orange and vermilion in the dark cavern of the hearth, and he added a few small logs then stood up, dusting his hands.

'What is this place?' The room was filled with nail-biting tension, raw, unsubtle, and Hannah felt like screaming, but her voice, amazingly, had emerged coolly enough.

He shrugged out of his coat, hanging it on a hook on a door that led to another part of the cottage, and he told her, 'The place I come to when I want to unwind. Secluded, lonely, no neighbours. And don't look so disgusted, it's quite civilised—running water, electricity. You won't have to rough it entirely.'

He'd mis-read her on that one. It wasn't disgust she was feeling, it was something akin to terror. And that was something she couldn't afford. Already she could feel the panicky surge of incipient hysteria and it would make rational judgement impossible. She needed all her wits about her if she were to get out of here with the only harm done the loss of a holiday.

It had been as if, in telling her of the cottage's isolation, he'd been warning her to expect no help from any other quarter. There were just the two of them, marooned together in a snowbound wasteland. She looked at his lean, muscular frame, the breadth and power of the chest and shoulders in the heavy sweater that exactly matched the colour of the nut-brown cords he wore, and the deep agony of fear held her immobile.

He was removing his wet shoes and socks and he glanced up at her, sideways, his eyes dark and unfathomable in the classic severity of his face.

'Give me your coat, and you'd better take those wet boots off.'

'No.' She was shaking inside, her mouth dry, and he walked towards her, barefooted on the soft deep-piled carpet, tall, powerful, entirely menacing, much too male.

Her breath was sucked in on a jerky hiss and he stopped, very still now, his eyes expressionless in a face that suddenly looked tired.

'Look, I mean you no harm. Can't you understand that?'

'Then why am I here?' She was backed against the door as far as she could get and she knew it was madness to show her fear because that was what he wanted and enjoyed, and like any other addict he would want more...and more...

'Believe me, I didn't want you here. But there was no choice. We couldn't have completed the journey, not in these weather conditions. So it's just something we're both going to have to put up with for a day or two. I'm going to make some coffee; we could both do with it.'

He sounded and looked so reasonable, yet she knew he couldn't be. She supposed it might be sound policy to leave things as they stood for the moment, not antagonise him, but she couldn't stop the words she flung at his retreating back.

'What journey? Where on earth were you trying to take me?'

He didn't answer, just walked soft-footed through the door he'd hung his coat on, and after a while Hannah felt her tense muscles relax enough to allow her to move away from the door.

Moments later she could hear him moving about above her head. At least she supposed it was him; there had been no evidence of anyone else in this place.

Rapidly, even though she knew it was useless because she'd seen him turn the lock and pocket the key, she tried the door. It was firmly locked, of course. She ran to the windows but they were fastened with security bolts.

The kitchen—panic was driving her now—there had to be a rear door, and from the small size of the cottage, as seen from outside, the kitchen had to lie beyond the door he'd just walked through.

It did. Hannah had just enough time to take in ochre-coloured walls, russet linen curtains at the single small window, a quarry-tiled floor, central table, a pine dresser and a wall clock that had stopped at a quarter past two before she heard the sound of his feet descending the pine stairs that led up from the side of a chimney alcove which now housed a streamlined electric cooker.

Frustration pounded in her temples and she jerked back into the sitting-room, closing the door and sagging against it, hauling herself together.

There had been another door, an outside door. All right, so she hadn't had the opportunity to try it, but assuredly it would have been locked. There was no way he'd leave her alone with an unlocked door, an unbarred window. He had gone to too much trouble to allow a careless oversight on his part to facilitate her escape.

Sighing, shaking inside with cold and fear and misery, she dragged a stool up to the hearth and sat there, staring into the leaping flames, huddled with the weight of her thoughts. She didn't hear him come into the room until his smoky voice penetrated the fog of her despair.

'You'd feel the benefit of the fire more if you could bear to be parted from your precious fur.'

She turned, presenting him with the back of her sleek dark head, the single heavy braid falling over one shoulder. She didn't want to have to look at him, to allow him to see the defeat in her eyes, then felt his sigh, as if it were her own, dragged from the depths of his being, and, seconds later, determined hands were removing the jacket.

Instinctively, she fought to retain her grip on the fur, but his strength, his determination, was too much for her and she watched with dull eyes as he hung it with his own on the peg on the door.

'Your boots.' Without waiting for any objection he was kneeling in front of her, one hand gripping her calf, the other tugging a wet boot from a frozen foot. And then, as if she'd been put into suspended animation, she watched as he took the slim nylon-clad foot between his hands, firmly but gently massaging, restoring warmth, circulation, feeling. And although she fought against it, she found the sensation oddly pleasant, and perhaps more than that as he spread her toes with supple fingertips, stroking, kneading... Her fixed gaze was on the top of his bent dark head, the crisp hair cut close to his skull, and the tingling feeling of warmth that was more than warmth, spread, lapping over her; although the tension was still there between them she knew it had subtly altered.

He raised his head then, as if sensing the change of mood, and she met the question that flared in his black eyes and something twisted deep inside her. Recognising it, disgusted by it, she dragged her foot from his now loosened hold.

'I can manage—thanks.' She bent down to tug at the other boot and he stood up, his voice brusque as he told her,

'I can't offer you any food until I've seen what's in the deep freeze, but I've made coffee.'

He'd brought a tray in, it was on a small table behind her, and she hadn't heard him bringing it in because she'd been deaf to everything but her own misery. But now she was fully alert again, her being suffused with a powerful awareness of this man as her enemy. He seemed even more dangerous now than he had done before. Her crazy reaction to his touch had told her that much.

Stiffly, she took the mug of coffee he held out, shaking her head when he offered her sugar. She was tempted to throw the hot liquid in his face and run, but there was nowhere to run. She couldn't walk through locked doors.

The coffee was strong and hot and black and she sipped it nervously, feeling his eyes on her. She said, not looking at him, 'You've made a mistake bringing me here. When I didn't turn up at the airport the friends I was meeting would have started to worry. By now they'll have checked with my flat, the cab company I was using...'

'You were travelling alone.' He sounded as though her attempts to make him think twice about the wisdom of keeping her here were boring him. 'On the seven-thirty-five flight out of Gatwick. The question of anxiously waiting friends doesn't come into it. So save your breath.'

He certainly hadn't skimped his homework. There was hatred in her eyes as she watched him drain his mug, set it down on the tray. 'There's work to be done if we're to be kept warm and fed,' he told her, turning to the door. 'Come with me.'

'Why?' If he expected her to hump fuel, or cook their food, then she'd see them both freeze and starve first. He turned, the mutinous flash of green eyes making his words come through his teeth.

'Because I want you where I can see you. Move.'

She was sorely tempted to stay exactly where she was, because if he wanted co-operation from her he wasn't going to get it. But her eyes had fallen on the fire irons—Georgian, she guessed—heavy.

Making her movements reluctant, but not reluctant enough to have him whipping round, dragging her behind him by her hair, she got to her feet.

As if satisfied, he turned again, going through the door, and Hannah bent down, her supple body moving swiftly, her right hand closing round the lethal poker, and she was right behind him in the kitchen as he walked towards the door on the far side of the room, his hand in a pocket, searching for keys.

Violence in any form was abhorrent to her, but she had no choice. Even so, subconscious reservations must have made her movements reluctant, sluggish, something of her deep unease transmitting itself to the tall, powerful man, alerting him, because he swung round on the ball of one foot, one hand lashing out to exert a killing pressure on her upraised arm, forcing her shaking fingers to release their hold, her eyes to widen, darken, as the heavy metal clattered on the red tiles.

'You've got an evil nature, lady.'

Strangely enough he didn't look angry, and certainly not surprised. And his words were flat, as if he knew it all.

'And what did you expect me to do?' She was trembling, ashen, her eyes brilliant slits of emerald, her voice a hoarse undertone as she rubbed her wrist where his fingers had bitten into flesh and bone. 'Thank you for so kindly bringing me here?'

He acknowledged her sarcasm with the almost imperceptible lifting of one brow. And the tension in the room built, wrapping around them, keeping her rooted to the spot. He possessed a powerful male beauty, but it was charged with menace, more terrifying because it was subtle, undefinable. It was a fiercely authoritative face, a commanding passionate mouth that twisted contemptuously as he looked down at her.

'I wouldn't expect you to give thanks for a cup of water if you were dying of thirst,' he grated. 'Your sort takes everything for granted. But I can see I'm going to have to tell you exactly why you're here, and where I was taking you—and why. Pity,' his mouth quirked bitterly, 'because I'd pinned my hopes on shock tactics; anything less would wash over your thick hide. But if I don't we'll never get a thing done and I don't intend wasting my time by watching you every second in case you're creeping up behind me, intent on murder.'

# CHAPTER THREE

THE man who called himself Waldo Ross pulled a leather-covered squashy sofa closer to the fire and dipped his head.

'Sit down, won't you.' His mouth moved wryly. 'This will hurt me more than it will hurt you.'

She sat, reluctantly; the sofa was made for two and he joined her. Edgily aware of him, she gritted her teeth. He was her captor, her tormentor, but now, more than even that, he was emerging as the complete alpha male.

She felt, and she adjured herself ruefully not to be surprised by this, that he was the only other human being in the wintry prison that was of his making. Almost, she could feel herself relying on him for her own sense of identity in a situation which was intolerably alien.

Shivering slightly, she tried to get her perspectives right. He was going to tell her why he'd done this, and it might be even worse than she'd imagined. He was leaning back against one corner of the sofa, his long legs stretched out, his hands loosely clasped.

He looked relaxed, but then he had no reason to be otherwise, Hannah thought sourly. But those black eyes were far from relaxed; intent, with a trace of underlying derision, they held her face, ready to judge her reaction.

'This was meant to be a one-day thing, but, as you know, the weather put paid to that. I was taking you to see Lottie Wilmott. After that you'd have been free to go, get another flight out to Morocco, go on with your holiday.'

'Lottie?' Her high smooth brow creased. This had to be the very last thing she'd expected to hear him say. Relief weakened her. So he really hadn't meant to harm her after all! Drawing in a wavery breath, her voice a thin and shaky whisper, her eyes on his face, she said, 'You didn't have to act like the Mafia. Why didn't you say Lottie wanted to see me? I would have gone any time.'

She had been fond of Lottie Wilmott. Eden's mother was a pretty, faded lady, too sensitive for her own good, and her husband, David, was an older version of Eden in looks, but with a stolidity of character that poor Eden would never have achieved. Eden had inherited his father's looks and his mother's personality. After Hannah had heard of Eden's death she had immediately visited Lottie and David in their comfortable farmhouse near Great Yarmouth. Lottie had been hysterical, laying the blame for the accident that had robbed her of a son firmly at Hannah's feet. Eden hadn't been able to get over Hannah's wicked rejection, and if he'd taken a drink too many on the eve of the wedding she'd called off, who could blame him? And if he hadn't been desperately unhappy, half-way inebriated, then his judgement wouldn't have been faulty, he wouldn't have had that smash. It was all Hannah's fault.

Hannah hadn't seen Eden's parents since then. There had seemed no point. Seeing them again would only upset them, particularly Lottie. But if Hannah had known the older woman wanted to see her she would have dropped everything and gone. She said again, more firmly, 'I would have gone, willingly, any time.'

'Oh, yes?' Disbelief, disgust, was patent in the twist of his mouth. 'You've been to see her once since Eden died, and then you couldn't leave fast enough.' He got to his feet, towering over her, his look dismissive. 'There was a time when she wanted to see you, but couldn't bring herself to ask because she knew you wouldn't want to bother. That was some months ago. Lately, she's gone beyond wanting anything. So making you see her was my idea. You're going to take a long, hard look at what you've done. It's time you faced up to the havoc women like you leave behind them.'

He was already at the door to the kitchen before she could sort out the confusion of her thoughts and make any response, ask the questions that needed to be answered.

He told her curtly, 'So now you know your precious skin's in no danger, you can help me get organised. I'll get enough fuel in to last twenty-four hours while you see to some food.'

'No.' He might have answered the dodgy question of her safety, settled her fears on that score, but he had presented other, almost as alarming issues, and he had ruined her holiday, put her through an agony of terror. If he wanted food he must get it himself.

'God, but you're stubborn.' The black look he gave her was denigrating. 'An accident of weather landed us here instead of Yarmouth, I've told you that much. But I'm not about to apologise, because in my book you deserve all you get. The fuel is all outside and the food is mostly in the freezer. We need to keep warm, to eat. I might have guessed you'd want everything doing for you.' His mouth curled cruelly. 'But I'm not Eden and I'm not Gerald Orme. So move.'

Hannah moved. If she didn't she knew he would make her, and she didn't want his hands on her. But she made sure her sleek head was held high, and her eyes were bright with boiling anger as she stalked past him, sweeping through to the kitchen as he moved aside in the doorway.

'Well?' she snapped mutinously. 'Where's this damned food I'm supposed to be cooking for you?'

'Through here.' He had brought his sheepskin with him and he shrugged into it, not looking at her, his face hard. Opening the door she had earlier believed led outside, he stepped through into a large built-on utility room, pushing his feet into wellingtons that stood by an outer door. Next to the capacious deep freeze were a small washing machine and a drier, so he didn't believe in roughing it entirely when he came here.

The outer door opened inwards, which was lucky; there were several inches of snow lying on the path outside with deeper drifts between the cottage and the shed she could just see through the continuing blizzard.

Hannah shuddered as he closed the door behind him, more from the effect he had on her than from the low temperature, then went resignedly to investigate the contents of the freezer. She took bread and a pizza and then, as an afterthought because the wretch would probably want her to make an evening meal, too, a couple of steaks.

Dumping the food on the kitchen table, she noticed he'd wound the clock. Almost one. She was hungry, now she came to think of it. Breakfast seemed a lifetime away, another world.

There was a portable Calor gas heater. She lit that, set the oven for the pizza and scouted round for a baking tray and cutlery, and found a cupboard stocked with dry goods, tinned food. Selecting a can of soup, she put it in a pan and put it on the electric cooker to heat up, her movements jerky and quick because of the anger that still rode her. He came through from the utility room, snow plastering his hair and his coat, his arms piled with logs, and he said, an inflexion of patronising amusement there, 'Still hopping mad?'

She swung round to face him, bitterness tightening her mouth, sharpening her voice. 'You've cost me a holiday I've been looking forward to for months, so you tell me why I shouldn't be livid!' But strangely, it wasn't the lost holiday that was in the forefront of her mind. He had lost her more than that. Her equilibrium, for one thing, and her self-respect, and she mourned both bitterly, because she was remembering the untenable feelings she'd had when he'd touched her, the quick excitement that had snaked through her as he warmed her frozen feet with his deft, strong, knowing hands...

'Tough.' He brushed past her on his way to the sitting-room with the logs, his voice coming bleakly. 'You've lost David and Lottie—particularly Lottie—a bloody sight more than a holiday.'

His riposte defeated her, the heat of her anger sliding away, leaving the void of cold uncertainty. She didn't know what he was talking about. It wasn't her fault Eden had died—if it was the loss of a son he was talking about. She had done her best for Eden; but he hadn't wanted to know.

And what was it to him, in any case? Where was the connection? It was something she had to find out because these veiled references were driving her out of her mind. He must have had her investigated very thoroughly to have come up with Gerald's name, the fact that they dated on occasion.

Soberly, she ladled soup into bowls and took the pizza from the oven, the cheese topping golden and bubbling. She told him flatly as he walked back into the room, 'Lunch is ready.'

They ate quickly, Hannah because, despite the horror of the morning, she was ravenous, and he because, no doubt, he wanted to get on with what he was doing outside before the light went. Afterwards, stacking the used crockery, she asked him, 'Who are you? What are the Wilmotts to you?'

His reply came evenly. 'Waldo Ross, I've already told you that, and the Wilmotts are my parents.' Which had to make him insane, or something.

'You're crazy,' she told him expressionlessly, moving the dishes to the drainer, turning on the hot tap. 'Lottie and David Wilmott had two sons, Donald and Eden. Eden's dead and Donald was in Hong Kong the last I heard. So which son are you, Mr *Ross*?'

'Simple.' His tone was infuriatingly calm. 'David and Lottie fostered me when I was nine. I gather they thought the name "Waldo" outlandish, so they called me Donald, but I prefer my own name.'

'So you are Donald!' That shook her; she hadn't expected anything like this. She turned off the tap and faced him. He was still at the table, lounging back in his chair, felinely elegant, his eyes on her. He looked coldly controlled, his face giving away nothing of what went on in his mind, and she knew, in that instant, what Lottie had meant when she'd said he was self-sufficient.

He was a loner; he walked alone through life, needing no one. He made his own rules and she was the victim of one of them.

'Waldo,' he reiterated, and Hannah shrugged. 'Whatever, it still doesn't explain why you took it into your head to abduct me, or why Lottie should want to see me now.'

'She doesn't, believe me.' He stood up, tall, powerful, his dislike of her a thing of shape and substance. She could feel it lying between them, heavy, sharp. He reached for his coat again, the discarded boots. 'Lottie doesn't care much who she sees or doesn't see now. Since Eden died she's become increasingly withdrawn. And as you killed her son as surely as if you'd put a bullet through his head, I'm going to make you face up to exactly what you've done.'

'I haven't done a thing!' The bitter menace in his voice turned her stomach, but she had too much pride to plead with him, to tell him he'd got it all wrong.

'Your sort never do, do they?' He moved to the door, his back broad, dismissive. 'You take all you can—love, devotion—then toss it away like a broken pot as soon as you're bored, never giving a damn for the emotional mess you leave behind. Well, just for once, I'm going to make sure you get to stare the consequences of your bitchiness in the face. I'll make sure of that, if it's the last thing I do on God's earth.'

Hannah didn't see him again until the light began to go. After she'd washed the dishes and replenished the fire with the logs he'd brought in she had curled up on the sofa, a prey to uneasy, confused thoughts.

Lethargy, the unwelcome aftermath of rage, drained her already tired body. Lottie had called her all the vile names she could put tongue to, but Lottie had adored Eden, so the abuse, though it had hurt, was not altogether surprising. She must have divulged her mistaken opinion of Hannah's character to Waldo and he, never stopping to think or ask questions, had barged right in like an avenging angel.

Only there was nothing remotely angelic about him. And there was little point in trying to walk out. The front door was locked and he'd see her if she tried to leave by the rear exit. Attempted escape would be a futile statement because he would be alert to the possibility.

She stirred uneasily, glancing over her shoulder to the window. Snow still fell thickly, plastering the panes, and she sighed, getting up, stretching, flicking on a table lamp and crossing to close the curtains against the gathering twilight.

Her supple body in the figure-hugging burgundy jumpsuit was poised, outlined against the window as she stiffened, hearing him come into the room, hearing the clatter of logs as he dropped them in the iron cauldron.

Hannah snapped the curtains across the rail and turned, her stance defensive. Her eyes were defiant, not dropping when he met them with his cool black stare. The look he gave her was sheer insolence, a summing-up that as good as stripped her.

As she considered attack to be the best form of defence, she jerked her chin up, exposing the long pure line of her throat, her voice barbed.

'So I broke my engagement to Eden, but you weren't around when it happened. You were in Hong Kong. So what gives you the right to set yourself up as judge, jury and executioner?'

'He was my brother. That gives me the right.' He fetched a bottle of whisky from a cupboard and dumped some into a tumbler, glancing up at her briefly from shadowed eyes. 'Want some?'

Hannah shook her head impatiently and he took his drink, straddling a chair, his eyes like chips of frozen jet in a face that was carved granite.

'Lottie and David gave me everything. A home, affection, a sense of who I am. They gave me a purpose in life. In fact, they are the only people who have ever given me anything—and I'm not talking about material possessions. And what you did to Eden, and the consequences of that, have turned a gentle, sensitive woman into an uncaring cabbage. That gives me rights.'

The implacable, unreasoning hatred she felt coming from him turned her cold. She walked out of the room, knowing that if she stayed she'd end up screaming at him like a fishwife—and that wasn't her style; she wouldn't demean herself.

She threw over her shoulder, tersely, 'I'll cook the steaks and then I'm turning in. I've had as much of today as I can stand.'

Hannah wasn't hungry, but making a meal would give her something to do. And as soon as she'd eaten she'd go to bed, get away from his bitter, hating presence and think about what to do.

Her ski-gear was in her suitcase and if she waited until he was asleep, went through his things for the door key, she could get out of here. She was fit and determined, above all determined; getting through the snow to some kind of civilisation wouldn't be a picnic but it wouldn't be completely out of the question.

He padded into the kitchen as she was putting the steaks under the grill, and, her mind on her plans, she asked,

'Where did you put my suitcase?'

'Upstairs. And if you want to use the bathroom it's left at the head of the stairs. You'll find your case in the bedroom on the right. I'll watch the steak.'

She found her case where he'd said it would be, at the foot of a king-sized bed which was pushed against a wall. The bedroom was large, cold, furnished with the barest necessities, but all good stuff; antiques of superb quality, no clutter. The room of a man who had no time for extraneous frills.

Hannah rummaged in her case for her washing things, remembered that they were in her flight bag and stumped downstairs again, ignoring his bland smile, but answering 'medium' when he asked her how she liked her steak done as she swept past him with her washbag. If he expected normal civilised behaviour from her then he would just have to think again.

Washed, her make-up carefully renewed because her confidence needed all the boosting it could get, she loped around the two rooms, checking the windows. As downstairs, they were fastened with security locks and she had no idea where to find the key. And why jump out of windows when she could walk out of a door? He kept the door keys in the pocket of the trousers he was wearing. She would find them when he was safely asleep.

Frowning, she stopped in her tracks and backtracked to the small landing at the head of the stairs, her worst fears confirmed. There was only one bedroom, so she was going to have to sleep on that small sofa, and at five foot seven inches she didn't fancy that. No matter, it would only be for one night, and only until she thought he'd had time to fall asleep. This time tomorrow she would be back at her flat—maybe with a seat on the next flight to Morocco already arranged.

Only—— She paused half way down the stairs. If he had taken her case up then he probably meant her to use the bed, and the thought of the discomfort he would endure on that sofa—he had to be six-foot-two or three— brought a satisfied smile to her face.

It was the first thing she'd had to smile about that day and she was still smiling when she went through the door at the foot of the stairs. He must have interpreted it as appreciation because he'd gone to much more trouble than she had at lunch time.

The table was spread with a tawny linen cloth, there was wine and he'd cut the defrosted granary loaf into chunks, putting them into a wicker basket. And the steaks on earthenware platters looked good, garnished with tinned tomatoes and frozen peas. She said stiffly, as he pulled a chair out for her and complimented her on her timing with a smile that would have melted the heart of any woman who didn't know him, know what he was capable of, 'I'm not hungry,' because she wanted to put him down. She preferred hostility from him to pleasantries, any day of the week.

'Suit yourself. If you can sleep on an empty stomach, fine. Who am I to argue?'

She sat at the table because it seemed stupid to stand, though she could have gone through to the sitting-room and left him to it, but she didn't think about that at the time. And what he'd said about sleeping on an empty stomach set her thinking. She wouldn't be sleeping tonight; she'd be walking in near arctic conditions, and it would be hours before she got her next meal.

Besides, the delicious aroma set her delicately sculpted nostrils quivering, her taste-buds responding. She'd need food inside her tonight, and she studiously ignored the 'I told you so' look he shot her as she picked up her knife and fork.

But she refused the wine he offered. She was bone weary already and the wine would make her sleep as soon as her head hit the pillow, and that mustn't happen.

'I know you're not a teetotaller,' he commented witheringly. 'Must you be so childish?'

She had been carefully holding herself in check ever since their last set-to, simply because there seemed no point in burning her energy in pointless argument. Whatever she said, he wouldn't listen, he had gone beyond listening where her involvement with Eden was concerned. He had his own preconceived ideas and he was sticking to them. But his taunt about her being childish when, given the circumstances, any other woman would have been raising the roof, got her on the raw.

Flinging her cutlery down, her careful control gone, her eyes a hating green glitter, she ground out fiercely, 'If there's a child's mind in an adult's body around here, mister, it's yours! You know nothing about me, nothing! If you did you wouldn't have brought me here.'

'I know you.' If he was angry he didn't show it. The harshly drawn lines of his face were impassive as he leant back in his chair, his wine glass in one hand, the other relaxed, resting on the cord covering of a tautly muscled thigh. 'I asked questions, dozens of them, and came up with the same answers. You're like a beautiful, greedy child—you'll suck a man dry emotionally without turning a hair, and then move on to get your kicks elsewhere. And you don't draw the line at married men, do you? Did you leave the Sages' marriage in ruins, or did Edward go back to his wife? I never did dig that deep, I didn't have the stomach for it. So tell me now—or didn't you bother to find out about a trivial matter like that?'

He tipped his glass and drank his wine, the strong muscles of his throat rippling, and Hannah hated him with a searing, burning hatred that went deeper than anything she'd ever believed herself capable of.

So he'd asked questions and come up with all the wrong answers and she loathed him too much to even begin to bother to put him straight. He'd delved that far back, had he? It didn't seem possible, and to cover the savage surge of revulsion she felt, she grated, 'You must have paid a bomb in detective agency fees. I hope you consider you got your money's worth!'

Without waiting for any reply he might make she pushed herself to her feet. She couldn't wait to get away from here, and on second thought she'd forget about trying to continue with her holiday and spend the time seeing lawyers. She would sue him if it was the last thing she ever did. She'd make him pay for this, and go on paying!

'I'm going to bed.' She stalked to the door. It was early but she wasn't staying down here for one second more, she'd start throwing things if she did.

There was a book in her flight bag, a good one, and that should keep her awake until he was asleep. And then she was getting out. Nothing would stop her.

He didn't say goodnight and she didn't expect him to. She went up the stairs, almost light-headed with relief because she wouldn't be seeing him again except, maybe, in court. She'd take his car keys, too, because she might just be able to back it down the lane. And if she couldn't she'd hurl them into the snow, where he wouldn't find them!

A hot bath relaxed her just a little and it used up some time, and she slipped into a bathrobe of his that was hanging on the bathroom door because she hadn't packed a robe of any kind and she'd be too uncomfortable in her ski-gear if she had to lie in bed for hours waiting until she could be sure he was asleep.

The soft towelling folds enveloped her, comforting her, but she would have preferred it if the fabric hadn't held the lingering scent of him—slightly spicy, slightly lemony. She would just have to ignore it.

Back in the bedroom she peered out of the window, checking the weather. It had stopped snowing and moonlight washed the lonely landscape in black and silver. A clear, frosty night; Hannah shivered, collected her paperback and burrowed under the duvet. But she couldn't concentrate on the printed page; her own drama was so much more immediate. The fact that Waldo Ross had dug deep enough to come up with Edward Sage had shaken her. And she was still shaking.

He'd put the wrong interpretation on what he'd discovered, created yet another reason to stain her character.

She had been just nineteen, still wet behind the ears, newly arrived in London to take up her first job—as a very junior secretary with a publishing firm. She and Edward Sage had shared the same bench in the park where she ate her sandwiches, they'd got talking, and a few days later he'd asked her to go with him to see a film they'd been discussing. He had been charming, good-looking, and he made her feel special, and it had only been a matter of time before she'd fallen in love. He had said he loved her and for Hannah, her innocence a clearly stamped brand, that meant marriage. She'd had it all planned, down to the last detail, with her father officiating and her mother proud and tearful in a smart new hat and herself in drifting white, carrying orange blossom.

Fortunately, those dreams had stayed locked away inside her head. Back at her bed-sit one night she had tearfully told him she wanted to wait until they were married because, by then, her blushing refusal to allow his kisses and caresses to go any further had resulted in an anger that had frightened and saddened her. It was then he had told her he was already married. He'd accused her of being a tease, and worse, and had walked out. She had never seen him again. And Waldo Ross accused her of being the guilty party! There was no justice—none at all!

Roughly an hour later she heard Waldo come up the stairs and go to the bathroom. If he was preparing to turn in then it wasn't a moment too soon because in spite of her angry thoughts on the injustices her tormentor was heaping upon her she was finding it almost impossible to keep awake. She had been up since just before four-thirty and her day, as her father would have put it, had been one of the trials that the Almighty, in his wisdom, had seen fit to put upon her!

The thought of her father brought a soft smile to her passionate mouth. She would never stop missing her parents, their warmth and their wisdom, but the pain of their loss had passed through the transitional period to become deep gratitude for the loving family life she had known with them.

She was warm and comfortable in the big bed, too warm and comfortable. After she'd heard him go back downstairs she would make herself read a chapter of her book and then get dressed and sit on the stairs until she judged he was asleep. That he wouldn't sleep well on the small sofa was a thought she refused to dwell on at this stage of the game.

She heard the sound of the bathroom door and allowed herself the luxury of settling back, only for a moment, just while she listened for him to go back downstairs and through the kitchen. But just as she was nicely relaxed she froze, rigid with outrage, as the bedroom door opened and Waldo Ross walked in, as cool as you like, naked except for a towel slung low around his lean hips.

'So that's where it is.' His black eyes fastened on what was showing of his bathrobe above the duvet, rising slowly to the exposed V of creamy skin, her flushed face, the dark hair spilling out against the pillows. 'You're wearing it.'

He padded across the room towards the bed, his bare feet making no sound on the exquisite Afghan carpet. Her mouth suddenly dry, Hannah's wide green eyes were fixed with apprehension on his magnificent torso, the broad shoulders tapering down to a narrow waist, lean hips and very long legs. The pelt of dark hair on his superb chest angled down intriguingly, contrasting dramatically with the low-slung towel which was startlingly white against the tanned smooth skin, the crisp dark hair.

'If you'll just get out,' she managed, her voice sounding strangely croaky as she tore her eyes from his near nudity to fix them on the foot of the bed. 'I'll pass your robe through the door.' Her fingers nervously drew the edges of the garment together just above her breasts, as if afraid he would drag it from her there and then.

'Keep it on if you're cold,' he said. 'But move over, it's freezing out here.' He was already loosening the towel he wore and Hannah screwed her eyes shut and screeched,

'Get the hell out of here!'

'No way.' He looked at her through narrowed eyes. 'Stop acting like the outraged virgin I know you're not and move over. Or do I have to make you?'

His voice held a threat that made her feel ill, but she met his eyes squarely, not daring to lower her own because he'd already tossed the towel over a chair, and although it had been scanty it had been something!

'You are not sleeping with me, so don't think it. If you come near me I'll see you behind bars for rape.'

'Who said anything about touching you?' The thin line of his mouth showed deep impatience. 'I intend to

sleep in my own bed, and don't worry, you're the last
woman on earth I would want to touch.'

'That sentiment is entirely mutual,' she growled, stung,
though not knowing why. She was already scrambling
out of bed. 'I'll use the sofa downstairs.'

'The hell you will!' Remorseless hands took her,
bundling her over the mattress to the far side of the bed
which was hard against the wall, and he followed, settling into the warm hollow she'd made. Hannah, bolt
upright and breathless, loathed him as she'd never
loathed anyone or anything before, and she said, her
voice dripping vinegar,

'If you wouldn't touch me if I were the last woman
on earth, as you with your customary charm so gallantly
put it, then why, in the name of sweet reason, may I not
sleep downstairs?'

He was silent for so long that she couldn't resist a
sideways look, peering at him round the glossy curtain
of her hair, and she saw the ghost of a smile touch his
chiselled lips before he reached out and extinguished the
reading lamp.

Her book fell to the floor with a heavy clunk, the bed-
springs creaked once as he settled himself, then he told
her, with a calmness she couldn't forgive,

'Because I couldn't trust you not to break a window
and get out. I intend to take you to Yarmouth and I
don't intend to have to wade through that stuff out there,
searching the drifts for an idiot. So lie down and stop
whingeing and let us both get some sleep.'

# CHAPTER FOUR

IT WAS deathly silent in the room, the only sound his deep, regular breathing. Hannah sat rigidly upright against the pillows, as close to the wall as she could get without actually climbing up it, staring at the patterns the moonlight made on the walls.

She hardly dared to breathe, let alone move, for fear of waking him. He lay with his back to her, warm and comfortable in the part of the bed she'd warmed up earlier while she crouched like a block of ice, her dignity in tatters. *Pig!*

When at last she thought his sleep was deep enough she would have to make a move. Having to crawl over the monster without disturbing him would make things a thousand times more difficult, but her ski-gear was on top of her case, ready to hand, and she could bundle it up and dress downstairs. Then she'd have to search for the keys. He certainly hadn't had them on him when he'd come into the room, that was for sure!

Her face flamed in the cold silvery darkness as she remembered the magnificence of his hard nakedness, the perfectly proportioned masculine body. And then he stirred in his sleep, as if the erotic nature of her unwilling thoughts had penetrated his dreams, disturbing him, and she held her breath. Did the wretch never sleep properly?

Silently calling him all the names under the sun and a few more besides, she waited, trying to still the tremors of cold and inner tension that shivered over her skin.

Then, when his breathing had become slow and regular again for what she judged to be ten hours but was probably only ten minutes, she began, very slowly, very tentatively, to move.

It wasn't going to be easy to climb over his large, stretched-out body and not wake him, and his taunt about not wanting to have to search snowdrifts for her hadn't exactly filled her with joyful anticipation for the ordeal that lay ahead of her. But best him she would. Or die in the attempt!

Edging herself carefully towards the foot of the bed, she froze, rump uppermost, as that hated voice, sounding fully awake, drawled, 'Don't fidget so, woman.'

Sagging in mortified defeat, Hannah gave up, for now, and crawled back up the bed. She wanted to scream! It could be hours before she dared make another move. The odious creature obviously slept with both ears and one eye open.

And she was so cold! Aching all over with the cold, and stiff from trying to hold herself rigidly motionless. Too weary to withstand the temptation of warmth and comfort, she eased her long legs down beneath the duvet and snuggled her head into the soft down pillow.

Waldo, of course, was taking up far more of the bed than was fair, and as poking him in the ribs and telling him to move over would only draw unwanted attention to herself, she gritted her teeth and endured the nerve-rackingly close proximity of that relaxed, naked male body.

The crisp cotton sheets smelt of herbs, fresh and tangy, and the duvet was warm, so warm, the man's body warmer...

\*     \*     \*

Hannah surfaced partially from a deep sleep and blinked. It was an effort to open her eyes at all. It was still dark in the room but the square of windowpane revealed a sky which was beginning to lighten. Oh, but she was sleepy, so warm and comfortable, and only vaguely, at the back of her mind, was the feeling that she should be doing something unpleasant. But the feeling soon slipped away, swallowed in the warm mists of contentment. And when she woke again the room was filled with a soft grey light, her body suffused with a languor that had nothing to do with sleep.

Waldo had moved, that was her first conscious sensation; his naked body was cradling hers, fitting round her, one arm flung over her, his hand somehow beneath the folds of her borrowed robe curved around the soft mound of her left breast, the swell of her right breast resting against his arm. And her sensitised skin was totally aware of the prickle of dark hair covering that arm, of the light, relaxed pressure of the hand that cupped her breast.

Quite alarming sensations unfurled inside her, spiralling upwards and outwards until they irradiated her entire body and she felt her breasts harden with arousal.

Hannah knew what was happening to her. If he could have this effect on her when he was asleep, how much greater would it be if he woke and became aware of this unknowing intimacy, committed in sleep!

The temptation to curve herself even closer into his body was intense, and shaming. How could she react this way to an unprincipled, bigoted cad! She wasn't a wanton and, since Eden, had put all thoughts of men and sex right out of her mind.

No man had had this effect on her since those heady days when she'd believed herself in love with Edward.

And he had been another unprincipled cad! Was she
destined only to respond physically to that type of man?
Heaven forbid!

Eden had never stirred her at all. The sexual side of
their relationship had taken a poor second place to a
kind of mental dependency on his part and a belief, on
hers, that they could achieve the sort of gentle, caring
commitment that had been the hallmark of her parents'
marriage. And Eden had been no cad; weak, but no cad.

Waldo stirred in his sleep, his fingers flexing over her
breast, and she held her breath, willing him not to wake,
not yet.

He had stated that she was the last woman on earth
he would want to touch, and he'd meant it. He believed
her to be a heartless, man-eating tramp, and if he woke
and found that he'd taken her into his arms during the
night, that the touch of his hands had aroused her to
shameless physical desire—and no way would he miss
that piece of evidence—then he would be disgusted with
himself and even more disgusted with her.

She had to get out of this shaming situation and, not
caring now whether she woke him or not, she wriggled
away from him, dragging the edges of the robe together
as she scrambled over his body. Her feet had barely
touched the floor when his wry comment arrested her.

'Do you always get out of bed like a stampeding
elephant?' He followed the drawled remark with a lazy,
'What's the weather doing this morning?'

She could answer neither taunt nor question. She felt
so besmirched by her body's mindless reaction to his
touch, by the entirely erotic yearnings he had unwittingly woken. And the profile she presented to him as
she rummaged through her suitcase for something to
wear was stubbornly mutinous.

'Hannah——' His tone was dangerously soft and her hands grew still, her clouded eyes drawn unwillingly to his, then shying defensively away as she saw that he had pulled himself up against the pillows, his powerful naked torso making her heart kick, her breath flutter in her throat.

'We're going to have to live in very close proximity for a day or two, so wouldn't it be easier for both of us if we were to achieve some kind of truce?' he continued to the back of her head. 'This enforced togetherness isn't something either one of us would have chosen, but don't you think it would make sense if we were to try to make the best of it?'

She had found the clothes she needed now and she stood up, the movement taut with a tension she felt might easily pull her to pieces. This mess was all his fault. He had forced her here, forced her to share his bed, and yet he could still loll there, in superior fashion, and mouth platitudes on the advisability of making the best of a totally untenable situation. How typically, typically *male*!

Not deigning to give a verbal translation of her rage, she swept out of the room, incensed almost to screaming point as she heard his following husky chuckle.

Dressed in snug-fitting grey velvet trousers and a soft thick-knit sweater that exactly matched the colour of her eyes, Hannah re-braided her hair carefully, applied make-up and hurried to get downstairs before he started banging on the door, accusing her of hogging the bathroom.

Her temper needed some outlet so she crashed around in the kitchen, lit the Calor heater, put bread in the toaster and made tea in a brown earthenware pot.

Waldo Ross was a creep! And if he thought a few psuedo-sage words from him would turn her into a simpering creature, all sweetness and light, forgiving everything and, 'No, Waldo, I don't mind about my silly old holiday, nor the terror you subjected me to, not one teeny-weeny bit, so don't you give it another thought,' then was he in for a big surprise! How could he expect her to forget all he'd done, prepare his meals, share his bed, and make pleasant conversation into the bargain?

She found a jar of honey in a cupboard and banged it down on the table. *Creep!* But despite her vehemence, a small unwanted inner voice told her that he wasn't that. Arrogant, domineering, insensitive, insulting, stubborn, impossible—but no creep.

Ashamed of herself, she vividly recalled her astonishingly wanton reaction to his touch, not an hour ago. Her body might be a traitor to everything her intellect told her, but it wouldn't respond to a creep!

Eden had once told her that Waldo had the devil's own way with women, and Hannah made a mental addendum that he could even turn it on in his sleep.

Burning colour crept over her face at that thought, and the thought that followed hard on the heels of that one sent the colour draining away, leaving her ashen. Had he been asleep? He had sounded remarkably awake when he'd accused her of getting out of bed like a stampeding elephant. Had he just been lying doggo, taking a sensual man's enjoyment from the closeness of a near naked woman in his bed? Had he witnessed the shameful arousal of her body?

It really didn't bear thinking about, and she sat down quickly, staring with revulsion at the slice of toast she'd dropped on her plate. Right on cue he sauntered down the stairs. He was freshly shaved and dressed in dark blue denims and a dark blue sweater and suddenly, for Hannah, the atmosphere closed in, became thick with unbearable tension. The room wasn't small but now the walls seemed to press closer, to gather in on her, her intense awareness of him making it seem claustrophobic.

He poured out the tea she had made, saying nothing, the tension obviously not touching him, but Hannah began to feel ill with it. Tears ached at the back of her eyes, tightening her throat, and she hated him!

She stood up, not wanting breakfast now, and walked to the window, her movements feeling uncoordinated, as if she were no longer in charge of her body, as if, somehow, she were in the process of an unwanted and completely incomprehensible change.

Outside, the smooth unbroken snow seemed to stretch for miles. His voice almost hit her, such was the shock of its impact in the silent little room, making her shoulder muscles clench as he remarked, 'No, it didn't go away in the night. I'm as sorry about it as you are. It's going to be days before this lot clears.' She turned blindly, not knowing where she was going, not caring, but jerking to a halt as he commented drily, 'You're looking extremely pale and interesting this morning. Didn't you sleep well?'

He was spreading honey on his toast, his fingers strong—a cruel graceful strength that turned her stomach. Those same fingers had curved around her breast. Was that what he was taunting her with? Was he putting her pallor down to frustration? He had had no compunction about letting her know that he believed her to be as wanton as the intolerable desires she had experienced earlier, so he would naturally think that she would be only too eager to throw herself at him, given the slightest encouragement, or given no encouragement at all, come to that.

But his next words left her in no doubt of what his reaction would have been if she'd been crazy enough to have stayed where she was in his bed this morning, letting him wake to discover how easily he aroused her.

'And you're looking very beautiful, of course.' He drained his teacup and refilled it from the pot. 'But looking beautiful is your stock in trade, isn't it? I pity the poor blind fools who can't see beyond it. How any man can get turned on by a heartless bitch is beyond me.'

Nothing fazed him. He was handing out insults with a bland urbanity that wouldn't have been out of place in a maiden aunt's drawing-room. He sickened her.

Bright colour returned to her cheeks, deepening the green of her eyes as she reminded him, 'You were the one who was talking about a truce, remember? You're going about it in a very funny way.'

'I knew anything as civilised as that was out when I heard you crashing around down here, when you couldn't bring yourself to eat breakfast at the same table.' He stood up, stretching lazily, not caring one way or the other whether they had that truce or not, and Hannah hastily averted her eyes. He was too male, too sexy, too dominant, and she hated him with an intensity that hurt.

She had to get away from him; the pain inside her was unbearable, and nothing, nothing at all, touched him. The ice-like veneer was thick, impervious; he could lash her with his tongue, diminish her, and it meant nothing at all to him.

'So if you still want to fight, then that's all right by me.'

His parting taunt followed her up the narrow pine stairs. She stared blindly at her reflection in the full-length mirror on the wardrobe door, not recognising the tautly featured ashen-white face that stared blindly back with feverish glittering eyes.

Biting her lips to convince herself that this was real, that she was real, that this wasn't all a dreadful nightmare, she turned to make the bed. It gave her something to do. She refused to think of how she had shared it with him. No way would she share it tonight. He would have to knock her unconscious and carry her up first!

Retrieving her book from the floor, she went slowly downstairs, reluctant to face him again yet knowing she must. But to her infinite relief there was no sign of him. He had lighted the fire in the sitting-room, though, and she could hear the sound of the axe when she went back to the kitchen to wash the breakfast things.

He was still splitting logs when she investigated the contents of the freezer in the utility room, the sound of the axe coming clearer there. Peering out of the single tiny window, she could see that he'd cleared a path to the shed where, presumably, the fuel was stored.

The rear door was unlocked and there was nothing to stop her walking out, but something—sheer lethargy, perhaps—held her where she was. Whatever... She shrugged, turning back to the freezer. It was crammed with food and she took out some rock hard chicken pieces and put them on the kitchen table to thaw. She would select vegetables later and maybe bring out another loaf. There was enough bread left to have with the canned soup, which was all she was going to bother with at lunch time.

Unconsciously, and without examining her motives, she had taken her share of the daily routine that meant survival in these conditions, and, that done, she made herself some coffee and took it and her book through to the sitting-room.

It was peaceful there, no sound but the crackle and hiss of the logs in the hearth, and she piled more on and snuggled down on the sofa to read. But soon the print blurred in front of her eyes, the trauma of the last thirty-odd hours catching up on her...

The room was almost dark when she woke, stiff and cramped. The fire was all but out, but the cauldron had been refilled with logs so he must have come in while she slept. Disorientated, she got groggily to her feet, selected a few small logs and put them carefully on the embers, poking out some of the dead ash, her lips twisting wryly as she recalled how she'd tried to brain him. But, as always, he had been one step ahead of her, his reactions superb, his thinking astute.

Collecting her coffee cup, she went through to the kitchen, flicking on lights. The bland face of the wall clock showed almost three-thirty, the sky beyond the window pane streaked with the pink and orange of the setting sun, casting a lurid light over the steel grey winter landscape. Shivering, although the room was warm, she set the oven, rinsed the thawed chicken and put the kettle on.

The light was almost gone so he'd probably call it a day soon, would be glad of a hot drink. Though why she should entertain such charitable thoughts in regard to him was beyond her. It was probably because she was still too bleary with the long hours of sleep to think properly.

She could hear no sound of the axe when she collected vegetables from the freezer, see no sign of him along the cleared path. Shrugging, she hurried back to the warmth of the kitchen, made tea and sat drinking it, cradling her cup.

This evening she was going to have to try to talk to him. Seriously talk to him. Despite her attitude of earlier that day—and that had been engendered more from embarrassment and self-disgust than anything else—she could see the sense in declaring a truce, trying to co-exist in tolerable harmony for the remainder of their enforced incarceration.

The chicken was golden brown, bubbling in its own juices, the table laid, the sweet corn and broad beans ready to put into simmering water, and it was five o'clock. Quite dark outside now, and still no sign of Waldo. The wind was moaning, hurling itself against the window, and she peered out, moving the curtains aside so that a track of light shone out over the snow, turning it gold.

Where in heaven's name was he? He couldn't still be splitting logs! In any case, she hadn't heard the axe all afternoon.

She left the curtains as they were, the light from the window a beacon. There was no denying the feeling of deep unease that gripped her, making her feel slightly sick. Had he had an accident? Injured himself with the axe? It didn't bear thinking about!

Scrabbling around in the dresser drawer, she located the torch she'd seen yesterday when looking for cutlery, grabbed her coat, and was at the back door before she had time to stop and wonder why she should worry about him.

She had the door open, was fumbling with the switch
of the torch, when his deep smoky voice came out of
the darkness, startling her. 'Going anywhere special?'

'Waldo!' Her heart kicked with relief and her flus-
tered, 'I wondered where you were!' wasn't passed over.

'Worried, sweetheart?'

Choking back the hot denial his sarcastic words provoked, she nodded, 'You'd been gone so long. I was
afraid you'd had an accident.'

The in-fighting had to stop, she could see that now;
it hurt too much. So complete honesty on her part was
the best policy if they were to pass the next day or so in
any sort of harmony at all.

One eyebrow was raised in disbelief, and he brushed
past her, bringing the scent of frosty night air with him
and that, or something else, made her suck in her breath
as he told her,

'Save your concern for this chap.' He was in the
kitchen now and the words 'What kept you?' died on
her lips when she saw the scrap of feathers he held in
his hands. The tips of his fingers were blue with cold
but he'd been trying to convey some of his body warmth
to the frozen robin.

'Is it dead?' Pity wrinkled her brow. The scarlet breast
feathers looked like a stain of rusty blood as the small
creature lay, unmoving, in the big man's hands.

'I don't think so. It wasn't when I picked it up. Hold
it while I fetch a box.'

Hannah cradled the robin in her hands as he went out
again, holding it close to the warmth of the heater and
she told Waldo, her voice carrying a thread of excitement as he returned with a cardboard shoe box, 'It
is alive. I can feel its heart beating.' That the tiny beat
was faint and erratic she didn't add. It was enough to

know that the little thing was alive, had a chance, enough to know that Waldo had cared.

'That's something,' he agreed with what had been going on in her head. 'There's a box of tissues in the bathroom cupboard. Fetch some, would you?'

The bird was put in the tissue-lined box in a corner of the wide sitting-room hearth where it was warm and quiet and dim, and Waldo, washing his hands at the sink, said, 'It has a good chance, now. I'm glad you didn't scream.'

'Why on earth should I?' During the last ten minutes they had worked in harmony, no harsh words, and it felt good. She couldn't imagine why he should have expected her to scream. What was there to scream about, for goodness' sake?

'A lot of women don't like handling wild creatures—especially if the creature in question appears to be dead.'

'Oh. You know a lot of women?' She put the vegetables into boiling water and reached down to take the chicken from the oven.

Waldo said appreciatively, 'That looks good. If you mean "know" in the biblical sense, then no, not too many. But I have been acquainted with quite a few who would have yelled blue murder if I'd asked them to hold a maybe-dead bird.'

He was rubbing his hands dry now, standing quite close to her, and his black eyes were warm, laughter lines crinkling at the corners. His eyes weren't completely black, she could see that now; there were tiny golden lights in the midnight dark irises that made them sparkle like gold-flecked jet.

While Hannah served the chicken Waldo opened a bottle of wine; tonight she wouldn't refuse to drink it. The kitchen was warm, a safe haven against the bitter weather outside, and she felt the gentle atmosphere curl round her like love.

She had started the day hating him and was ending it with unreasoning contentment. Her stomach rumbled with hunger pangs as he accepted his plate from her, smiling. 'Me, too, I'm famished.' It was the first real smile she'd had from him, and it overwhelmed her. She sat down, weak from more than hunger, as he continued, 'I came in about one, wondering if you'd made lunch, but you were asleep by the fire.'

She started to eat, her eyes narrowing as he told her, 'I didn't want to disturb you; you were obviously catching up on lost sleep. My bed not comfortable?'

Hannah didn't want to talk about that; she didn't even want to think about it. And she didn't care for the glint in his eyes. Must he keep on referring to last night's sleeping arrangements? Ignoring the question, she popped a bite-sized piece of chicken in her mouth, 'You could have heated a can of soup for yourself.'

He shrugged, 'I could have, but I didn't. I went to take a look at the car, but it's wedged in about three feet of snow.'

He sounded really regretful, as if he couldn't wait to get out of here. And she didn't know why that should bother her. It didn't, not really, she consoled herself. It was unflattering, that was all, but his attitude towards her could hardly be called flattering at the best of times. And this was one of the better times.

'I met old Len Watkins down the lane. He'd been looking for sheep,' he told her, unaware of the confusion of her thoughts, for which she was entirely thankful. 'The snowploughs have been out but it will be ages before they get around to this track. This is the only house along here so they're not going to make the access lane first priority. But Len said he'd heard a forecast and there's a thaw expected in a couple of days.'

Which meant they'd be able to leave. A couple of days—time enough, surely, for her to convince him that she wasn't what he thought she was. Though why she should bother about his opinion, good or bad, when the damage had already been done, her holiday ruined, was something she didn't stop to think about.

The wind had ruffled his hair and that, and the mellow light, made his face seem softer in a faint blurring of the classically severe lines, angles, planes. But that didn't mean that he didn't look all man; hard, ruthlessly determined when he set out to get what he wanted. Which, at the moment, was a confrontation between herself and Lottie. The ridiculous part of it all was that had Lottie or David written and asked her to get in touch, then she most certainly would have done.

So what could Lottie have told Waldo to make him see abduction as the only way of getting her to Yarmouth? Nothing good, judging by the insults he had hurled at her!

Feeling his eyes on her, she glanced up, her long slender fingers twisting the stem of her wine glass. He topped it up from the half-empty bottle and leaned back in his chair, his dark eyes shadowed.

'Do you enjoy your job at the agency? I'm told Roger Orme is a high flyer. Does Gerald take after him in that respect?'

'Gerald's a hard worker, conscientious, but he doesn't have his father's flair.' She answered his question at face value. This morning she would have told him to mind his own damned business. 'And I love the work. It can often be routine, of course, but it has its moments—like finding an absolute gem in the dross of the unsolicited pile.' Her deep green eyes held a sparkle that was immediately extinguished by his response.

'Like Eden's first book?'

The tone he used, ever-so-slightly-iced-over, and the subject matter, sent a warning signal down her spine.

'I didn't handle that.' Carefully, she kept her voice level, calm. If he wanted a fight she wasn't going to give him one, but the tension was building inside her again. If he was ever going to see her as she was—blameless in the whole miserable affair—then she would have to act and look as though she were, and not jump on the offensive. 'Roger did. I tried to help Eden with his second. Roger had been away with 'flu when Eden phoned in. He was having problems; we had lunch—to discuss them. That's how I met him.'

'And the second book never got finished,' Waldo injected smoothly, too smoothly. 'Lottie and David were immensely proud of his first, looking forward to seeing his second in print. But he never wrote the second, did he? What happened? He got part-way through then ran up against you. Couldn't he keep his mind on his work with you around? Were you too much of a distraction?'

'Not at all.' It had been nothing like that. As time had gone on she had done all she could to boost Eden's fragile self-confidence. His second book wasn't taking shape and she'd agreed to meet him often, to help him over difficult patches. In her mind he was the antithesis of Edward. Edward had been the dominant one, his slightest frown sending her into trembling despair, his slow, secretive smile capable of raising her to the heights of dizzy ecstasy. She had been dependent on him, like a drug, but Eden had been touchingly dependent on her.

Perhaps now was as good a time as any to make Waldo see how it had been. Eden hadn't had a second book in him.

'It wasn't like that,' she told him, trying to sound convincingly matter-of-fact, but her voice coming stiffly for all her best efforts.

'No?' He, too, was maintaining a polite and civilised façade, as if this were merely an academic topic, of only marginal interest to either of them, one on which they held vaguely differing opinions, and not something that had given birth to his deep loathing of her and the woman he thought she was.

She knew it was useless. He would never believe she wasn't a self-centred bitch. So the only thing to do, to avoid another hurtful argument, was to change the subject. Collecting the used plates, she took them over to the drainer, her voice politely interested, but pitched a little too high.

'What do you do for a living? Something out in Hong Kong, isn't it?'

'All over—far east, middle east, India. And what do I do?' His tone had changed; it was rough velvet now, abrasive yet soft. 'Let's see how I can dress it up for your consumption. Call me a speculator—or perhaps wheeler and dealer might suit your image of me better. And don't change the subject.'

His voice was explosively harsh, the violence in it shocking her, keeping her rigid, afraid to move, her back to him.

'Were you too much of a distraction for Eden?' He savagely echoed his earlier question. 'He was too gullible when it came to women, too trusting when it came to you. My God! I could have handled you!' His fist cracked against the table and the sound reverberated through her skull, sending her pulses skittering out of control, raising the fine hairs on the nape of her neck.

He was behind her, close, and she couldn't turn because the hatred she could feel coming from him was getting to her, tearing her apart, in a way it hadn't done until now.

'Did you realise, then, a month before you'd promised to marry him, that you'd actually killed the goose that laid the golden egg? That his pain—the pain of loving you until it was an obsession, of having to share you with other men—had destroyed his creativity? Was it then that you called it off and moved on to find another, sleeker, fatter candidate for the dubious honour of sharing your matrimonial bed? I take it,' he ended with savage disgust, 'that Gerald Orme isn't measuring up to your high financial expectations? Hence the brush-off I heard you giving the poor sucker!'

For long self-condemning moments Hannah couldn't answer. The hatred, the penned-up violence coming from him froze her mind. He could change mood as quickly and completely as a chameleon changes its colour, and she couldn't cope with it.

Yesterday she would have swept out of the room, not deigning to waste her breath in reply to these fantastic misapprehensions of his. Yet now, something held her there, the wall of his disgust something she wanted to break down. But, as his hands touched her shoulders, searing her, the pressure of his hard fingers directing a jolt of electrifying sensation to each and every nerve end, her voice came at last, low and harsh, 'Don't touch me!'

She did turn then, lashing him with her eyes. 'You won't listen to the truth because you don't want to. It's not what you think, but you'll never believe me in a million years because you've got a closed mind. A

warped mind. You only believe what you want to believe. And for some twisted reason you revel in thinking
the worst of me. It is only me? Or do you think all
women are tramps?'

Briefly, his eyes were shuttered, his face hard, the lines
deeply indented, and then he bit out, 'Then tell me. Tell
me the truth—if you know the meaning of the word.'
His black eyes pinned her with steady derision. 'Tell me
your version of the truth. I'm in just the mood for a
bedtime fairy story.'

# CHAPTER FIVE

'AND will you tell Lottie the truth when you see her?'

They had moved to the sitting-room and Waldo had replenished the fire, checking on the bird. In the leaping fireglow, the only illumination there was since neither of them had bothered to put lights on, his face looked satanic. How could a man who showed so much concern for a feathered victim of the bitter weather be so implacably cruel when it came to his dealings with a fellow human being? The answer escaped her, and she sighed.

'The truth?' She wondered if he knew about Eden. He probably did. They had been brought up together in a close family unit. He must have known.

'What else?'

'Do you always tell the truth?' she evaded, playing for time, time to judge how much to tell him; to discover, if she could, how much he already knew about the brother he so clearly mourned and missed.

'Why not?' He countered her question with one of his own.

'Even if it hurts?'

'Of course. People have a right to the truth; it's no use living in a fool's paradise.'

The hard man had spoken. Hannah stared into the flames. Tell the truth and shame the devil? No matter that the knowing of it would create a new grief, a regret there was no expunging?

'How close were you and Eden?' Rather than join him on the small sofa, she had elected to sit on the hearth, holding her hands to the fire. But now the heat was getting through to her and she thrust herself to her feet, the grace of her movement unconscious. But she knew his eyes were on her as she prowled the room, the furniture unfamiliar in the flickering light, the shadows deeper, the darkness in the corners more intense.

'Closer than most true brothers, I'd guess.' His voice came at last, almost reluctantly, as if his life, his feelings, had nothing to do with the subject in hand. But he told her, nevertheless, his deep smoky voice seeming to bind them together in this silent, isolated place. 'I was nine when David and Lottie took me in—— Look,' his voice was edged with impatience, 'can't you stop prowling? You're like a caged tiger.'

Not the tiger, she corrected him mentally, edgily, I'm the prey, trapped in this cage with a human predator. The mental image conjured up thoughts that weren't easy to live with, but she did as he suggested and carried a stool to the hearthside, facing him, yet not looking at him, staring instead into the fire.

He told her, 'Having a family, people who wanted me, was a new experience. Eden was five years younger than me; he rather tended to hero-worship me. And I took care of him. Knowing I had someone to care for, as well as being cared for myself, helped me to find my identity.'

So if Eden had been his junior by five years, that made Waldo thirty-six. Strangely, the information was precious, and she prodded.

'And when you were both older?' She could sense the anger building up in him again but she needed to find out because it was important, it would affect the way she told him the 'truth' he had promised to listen to.

'We drifted apart, inevitably I suppose.' There was regret in his voice, a shadow of pain in his eyes. 'I was striking out on my own, enjoying using my brain. I needed to achieve something in my own right, not stay around helping David on the farm.' He fell silent, his eyes inward-looking and Hannah could feel his regret as if it were her own.

She asked, bringing him back to her, 'Where did you go? What did you do?'

'France.' The tone was clipped now, the past, and whatever it held for him, relegated to where it belonged. 'I began with a firm of estate agents and auctioneers, learned a lot, went to north Africa and set up on my own. A few big commissions in the antique world took me to India, back to Italy, and eventually out to the Middle East. By then I was shipping carpets to Europe and the States, dealing in property. While Eden was cloistered in Cambridge I built myself a financial empire, covering half the globe.' He shrugged, the movement of his wide shoulders almost insouciant. 'Eden was the dreamer, the academic, and all I had was a drive to succeed which was the most important thing in my life. We corresponded, of course—a couple of times a year on average—but we rarely met. I saw very little of my family after I was twenty. Until Eden's death brought me home.'

'And then you began to feel guilty,' Hannah remarked astutely. She had heard the regret in his voice, seen the pain in his eyes. Had he known of Eden's problems? Did he feel that had he been home more often, taken more interest in the brother who had tended to hero-worship him, then he could have helped, prevented a tragedy? She knew that what she was doing was cruel, but if he were to see her in a different light he first had to face up to his own shortcomings.

'You used them,' she went on, even-toned. 'You took all they had to offer—a home, security, love—and went. You were too busy building your empire to check up on what was going on back home.'

His eyes narrowed. She could see the brilliant glitter of jet in his shadowed face. He reached for the glass of wine he'd brought in with him, draining it, setting it back on the small table beside him with an angry click.

'Why the hell should I feel guilty? They all knew how I felt about them; and we're not discussing my shortcomings. So tell me what happened between you and Eden. Tell me why you jilted him!'

His voice castigated, but the shivers that rippled over her skin weren't due to fear of him. The worst part of this crazy episode was over, had been for some time, the part when she'd been frightened for her life. She wasn't afraid of him now; at least, she told herself she wasn't, because if you can make yourself believe something enough it becomes the truth.

And maybe that was what had happened for him. He had believed whatever it was Lottie had said about her because Lottie and David had given him everything. He trusted them. He felt guilty. So he would unquestioningly believe anything Lottie said. And his anger at the waste of Eden's life, a life he had been no part of for many years, had imprinted that belief indelibly on his mind. The rest was history.

She relaxed a little on the stool. Perhaps he would listen to, and believe, her version of the truth. Since Edward, and up until a day ago, she'd run her life the way she wanted it to go. A successful absorbing career, with no messy emotional involvements, her integrity unquestioned. Everything planned, worked out. Even her engagement to Eden had been considered carefully, the possibilities minutely weighed, the break clean and irrevocable when it came because the future as Eden had made her see it, finally, had not measured up to her precise expectations.

And then this silent, watchful man had broken into her life with the impact of exploding dynamite, altering her perceptions, the way she saw herself.

Her unforgivable mistake had been in agreeing to marry Eden in the first place; she could see that now. She hadn't loved him, or only as a valued friend. The possibility of passionate love, and the vulnerability, the dependence that inevitably went with it, had held no charms for her since her disillusionment over Edward Sage. It frightened her.

She and Eden, or so she had foolishly believed, could have shared a marriage based on friendship, trust, and the quality of caring. She had believed it could echo the tranquillity of her parents' marriage. But she had been wrong, so wrong. What she had failed to see was that her parents' marriage had encompassed a passionate love—and the rest, the quiet contentment, the devotion, had grown out of that.

Perhaps she could make Waldo understand, if not condone, the crime of promising to marry a man she had known she did not love, could never love in the fullest sense of the word. But she had never driven Eden crazy with her promiscuous behaviour—he had to believe that, too!

She wanted his respect, his understanding, and that need had slid slyly up on her, taking her unawares.

'I don't know what Lottie told you, but I can make an educated guess,' she began, staring into the flames, acutely conscious of him, every nerve-end excruciatingly attuned to his nearness. 'But she was wrong.'

She heard the sudden sharp pull of his breath, felt her own lungs expand, tighten, as if they shared the same nervous system.

'Are you saying Lottie is a liar?' The tone was almost casual and she turned her head, the heavy braid of her hair falling over her shoulder. His face was remote, closed. She could only guess at what went on in his head.

'No.' The word was a thin skein of sound, reaching out to him, trying to hold him. 'Not a liar. Mistaken. Eden obviously gave her the wrong reasons for the breaking of our engagement.' He wouldn't have given the right ones; there was nothing more certain than that.

But Waldo derided, 'Why should he do that? The man loved you. Why should he lie about the agony of knowing you'd never loved him, had graciously condescended to marry him because, at that time, you believed his books would make a small fortune, if he could keep repeating his first success? But he couldn't, not after he found out you were amusing yourself with other men and fully intended to continue to do so, even after the marriage. Yet, despite knowing all this, the poor sucker still wanted you, believed you would change. You killed his creativity, his drive to work, and just as surely as you were responsible for his death. Tell me,' he ground out viciously, 'did you ever love him?'

'No.' The flat monosyllable came quietly, and it was the truth, though she knew only too well how the single word would damn her in his eyes. 'Not in the way you mean,' she struggled to tell him, her voice thick, the words difficult to form. 'I was very fond of him, I respected him—his talent—the man I thought he was. I believed I could see a good future——'

'Until you realised he couldn't write, wasn't going to follow that first bestseller with dozens more!' he bit out, slicing into her attempts at an explanation of how she'd seen her future, and Eden's, as a carbon copy of the quiet devotion of her parents' marriage.

He moved, suddenly, and she thought he was going to strike her, but he went over to pour whisky into his glass, his shoulders tight with the effort of restraining himself, of not lashing out at her physically.

'You don't know the meaning of love. Your sort only loves number one, and that's an empty, pathetic emotion. And the only way to penetrate your thick hide is to show you the human misery you've left behind. And after you've seen Lottie you can go to the devil for all I care— for all anyone cares, as far as I know. And I hope, I just hope, that something gets through, that there's a conscience somewhere behind that beautiful empty façade. Because if there is, it's going to give you hell!'

He slammed the empty glass down and Hannah got shakily to her feet. She couldn't stand much more of this. He had loved the family who had taken him in, even though, on his own admission, he had seen little of them during the past sixteen years. And he still cared deeply about the woman who had mothered him. And he believed Hannah herself directly responsible for the way Lottie was now. Even if she told him the truth about Eden, he wouldn't believe it.

'As soon as we can get out of here I'll go to see Lottie,' she told him woodenly, flinching at his taut come-back.

'Too right you will. That's the only reason you're here.'

There was stark murder in his eyes, but she was more afraid of her own slipping control than she was of him. She had to stay calm, live through the next day or so as best she could. She must not be the one to light the fuse of an anger that could destroy them both. The tension between them had reached explosion point so she, at least, had to stay calm; the emotional storm, if it finally broke, would be devastating.

He looked pale, the lines of his face etched harshly, the dark eyes glittering as if with fever. Hannah's breath caught in her throat, her eyes sliding away from the intentness of his, dark sweeping lashes shadowing them.

'Are... Are there any spare blankets anywhere?' It was difficult to speak; the atmosphere between them seemed too heavy to breathe.

'Why? Cold in bed last night?' His curt reply didn't help.

'No.' She didn't want to think about last night, about the way they'd been when she had woken. It wasn't an episode she wanted to remember, and her face was almost as pale as his as she told him flatly, 'I'm sleeping down here tonight. On the sofa.' There had to be extra blankets somewhere, but if he wouldn't tell her she'd make do with her jacket. And she had to get out of this room, have a bath, anything——

He caught her arm as she passed him, jerking her to a standstill.

'I told you why I wanted you in my bed.'

As coolly as she could, she looked at the hand grasping her arm, the knuckles white with the pressure he was exerting, and then she raised her eyes to his. And no way must he see the way his touch, his nearness affected her.

'Let me go.' Her voice was calm, cold, giving no inkling of the turmoil inside her. And slowly the pressure of his fingers relaxed until she was able to wrench her arm free, rubbing it. She would have bruises for days, but the impression he'd made on her senses would take much longer to fade. He wasn't to know that, though,

and she averted her head, her tone deliberately
reasonable.

'I've told you I'll willingly go to see Lottie. And if
I'd been going to make a run for it I could have gone
today. The back door was unlocked; I could have walked
out and you wouldn't have known I'd gone for hours.'

'You were on your way out when I got back,' he reminded her, his mouth curling derisively at her rapid,

'I was going to see if I could find you.'

She turned away from him, pacing restlessly. She
wished he hadn't brought that up. She could have
sneaked out at almost any time during the day. That she
hadn't was entirely illogical, and she wasn't used to messy
thinking, not from herself.

'So you didn't run.' She heard the jar of the neck of
the whisky bottle against glass and thought, I hope he
isn't aiming to get drunk, then denied the idea. His
control so far had been superb; he knew exactly how far
to go. He wouldn't get drunk.

'So why the sudden aversion to sharing my bed? I
didn't touch you, and even if I had I doubt if you'd have
objected.'

That little gallantry stopped her in her tracks, her fists
clenched at her sides as shaming colour flooded her
cheeks. He had touched her and, far from objecting, she
had had to exercise a great deal of willpower to remove
herself from his unknowing embrace! She had been so
close to turning in his arms, holding him, waking him...
And that was something he must never be allowed to
know, either...

'I would rather sleep in a coal shed,' she said through
clenched teeth, her arms wrapped tightly around her
slender body as if physically restraining the need to
scream, to hit him.

'I wonder why.' He moved with a fluid masculine indolence, stationing himself between her and the door as if he'd read the message of intent in her eyes. 'They say all cats look alike in the dark, and you must have lost count of the times you've slept with a man, so why draw the line at me?'

'Because you don't turn me on, you creep!' The hot defensive words were out before she could check them, their implication clear. He already threatened her far too much without her taunting him with the lack of virility, lack of a sexual attraction he certainly did possess. He closed in, smoothly, silently, and she knew what was going on inside that well-shaped skull; it was there in the glitter of his eyes, in the tell-tale muscular spasm along his clenched jawline, and she backed away.

'Don't come near me, you bastard!' Her fingers scrabbled over the surface of the table at her back, searching for something to throw.

She hurled the heavy pottery vase when he was within two feet of her and he ducked his head, fury in his eyes as his hands snaked out. But she was gone, twisting on one heel, breaking past him for the door.

Clarity of thought was impossible in the panicky state she was in as she scrambled up the stairs, hearing him pounding up behind her. The bathroom—she could lock herself in! Her feet skidded on the rug at the head of the stairs and she pushed frantically at the closed door, thrusting it open and hurling herself inside.

But even as she threw herself against it, scrabbling frenziedly for the bolt, it jarred back on its hinges, sending her flying across the floor space, her eyes deep pools of drowning fear as she stared up at the angry man filling the doorway.

He was breathing heavily, the veneer of civilisation
stripped away. She had been afraid of triggering the response that would shatter his control, and cursed herself
furiously for losing her temper and taunting him with a
lack of virility.

His control had gone now, she saw that, saw the dark
intent in his eyes as he moved towards her. She tried to
speak but no words came, her throat constricted with
something more than fear, her heart thudding heavily,
painfully.

And as his hands reached for her, pulling her against
the hard length of his body, it was as though this
closeness offered a release from the devils that were riding
them both, as if the touching of their bodies was a con-
summation, bringing relief to the tensions that had
mercilessly flailed them.

The tension that had existed between them from the
first had finally reached fever pitch, exploded, trans-
muting to something else. There was tension still, she
could feel it coiling tightly inside her, see it in the raw
tensing of his jaw, in the glitter of his eyes. But it had
changed, subtly altered, touching some deeply feminine
instinct, a primitive and undeniable female awareness of
the male.

It was then that his mouth took hers, brutally at first,
as if he were intent on stamping his mark on her, as if
there were a pent-up need in him that could only be expressed by savage domination.

Hannah couldn't breathe, couldn't fight to extricate
herself, her total awareness concentrated only on the
pressure of his mouth against hers, the giddying sensation of a nameless need that was heightened to near
agony by his unmistakable arousal as his hips pressed
deeply against hers. She felt as though her entire being

had changed to a heavy fluid, totally receptive to the mind-blowing sensations that coursed through her, unlike anything she had ever experienced before.

And then, as if he sensed the receptive response she was unknowingly transmitting to him, the pressure of his mouth altered, his hands gentling, sliding around her to reach beneath the sweater she wore, his fingers trailing over her skin until she felt she was on fire.

Her lips parted mindlessly beneath his, allowing him access, and a low moan was torn from her as she met his probing tongue. Her hands crept up against the soft wool of his sweater, tentatively exploring the hard muscle and bone beneath before curling around his neck, her fingers splayed in the thick dark warmth of his hair.

Slowly, expertly, his hands caressed, sliding down to the narrowness of her waist and then moving seductively upwards, fingers feathering her ribcage, his exploration deliberately sensual, tormenting.

And then, with no opposition from Hannah, who could no longer think coherently, he was removing her sweater, unclipping the silky bra, both garments dropped to the floor unregarded as his eyes devoured her body.

'My God—you are beautiful!' The words were torn from him, as if the admission were against his will. She registered the harshness of his breathing and then was completely lost as his hands slid up to cup her breasts and his head lowered to take one rosy peak to his mouth, and then the other.

Reality was gone, it had been lost since the moment their lips had met; her body became a willing slave to his passion and her lashes drooped heavily, languorously, as she watched the dark, well-shaped head as he hungrily suckled.

Nothing remotely like this had ever happened before, not with Edward and certainly not with Eden. Her feelings for Edward had been those of a romantic schoolgirl, entirely ignorant, the stars in her eyes blinding her to the realities of more basic needs. And her relationship with Eden had been almost platonic, warmed to life only by what she now perceived had been a brand of maternal protectiveness.

But this was real, basic, as old as time, and even as he took her boneless body in his arms and carried her through to the bedroom, his breath a husky caress against her ear—'Now tell me I don't turn you on!'—nothing could slake the fever he roused within her, nothing but desire's natural conclusion.

She wanted him with a raging need that overruled everything else. It was madness, the tiny part of her brain that was still functioning reminded her as he laid her on the bed, removing the rest of her clothes, but that thought expired, slipped away quietly, and she lifted her arms to him, her body on fire with the need only he could satisfy. She heard his harshly indrawn breath, felt the weight of his body on the mattress beside her, and then the burning touch of his mouth as he lingeringly caressed every inch of her with his lips.

'Touch me!' His voice was hoarse and the command triggered an instinctive, unstoppable response in her as, shyly at first, and then more boldly, her hands trailed over the silky skin that clothed hard muscle and bone.

He wrenched out of his sweater and she felt him shudder as her fingers shamelessly found the zip of his trousers and then, out of nowhere, a cold spasm of fear gripped her, stilling her hands, freezing her blood.

It was nothing like the fear she'd experienced when she'd realised the fact of her abduction. That had been hot and dark; this was chilling. And she knew that if he made love to her now she would, in some indefinable way, be forever bound to him.

She was far from being promiscuous; if she had been it might be different. The sense of morality, instilled by both parents, the need for personal integrity, would not permit the ultimate act of physical love without the accompanying commitment of spiritual love.

Desire, born of rage, was no viable substitute; it would cheapen them both.

'It's too soon,' she whispered huskily as he lay beside her, half covering her, his nakedness, his full arousal, magnificent. She still wanted him, achingly, God, how she did, but her sense of self-worth went deeper, its roots firmly in her upbringing, her own deep-seated conviction that sex without love was worthless, a mere functional coupling of mindless bodies.

'You are driving me wild.' His voice was a low groan of protest, misreading her. 'You've been steadily driving me out of my mind since the first time I saw you.' He cupped her face in his hands, his eyes probing her soul. 'I know what you are and part of me, God help me, despises what you are. But you're a fever that won't give me peace!'

Slowly, his head descended, his lips nuzzling the vulnerable hollow at the base of her neck, his fingers trailing the softness of her waist, the jut of a hip bone, moving to discover the soft mound of her femininity, finding his answer.

'You want me, too, Hannah. Your body doesn't lie.'

He was right, of course he was right, but she could not, would not, give herself in the act of love for the first time to a man who despised her, to whom the words 'commitment' and 'love' in regard to herself were a joke.

And even as his fingers scorched her, bringing the beginnings of a spiralling ecstasy she had never known before, she twisted away, rolling to the floor and clambering shakily to her feet, her breath coming in uneven gasps, the pain, low inside her, a revelation of her body's frustrated needs.

'Waldo, I can't——' she offered, the feeble beginnings of a plea for understanding from him in this moment, useless. There had never been, and probably never could be, a single moment of understanding between them.

Clutching what she could find of her discarded clothing to her, to hide her nudity, she faced him, her heart twisting painfully as she became aware that he, too, was suffering.

He lay rigid, not moving, the sinews and muscles of the long hard body corded with tension, his face a white mask, the glitter of black, burning eyes emphasising the frightening pallor. She put out a hand to him, hopelessly offering what she could of comfort, of sympathy, but his words flailed her.

'Is this a sample of how you drove Eden crazy? Get out of my sight, you beautiful bitch, before I make you wish you'd never been born!'

# CHAPTER SIX

HANNAH dressed hurriedly in the bathroom, picking her discarded sweater off the floor with shaking fingers, blaming herself for what had happened. She should never have allowed things to get so out of hand.

His firmly held yet erroneous impression of her character had instigated that initial kiss. His rage over her unthinking taunt had finally broken through his control, exploding the tension that had been between them all along until, for him, it had become a case of kissing her or hitting her.

He was a highly sexed virile male and he had found a willing, responsive female in his arms—a female, moreover, whom he believed to be entirely promiscuous. What more natural vent for boiling emotions than the catharsis of the ultimate sexual act?

But she should have had more sense, been alert to the dangerous aftermath of flashpoint; she should have had more self-control. Instead, her body had been a willing pupil to his sensuality and now, by her rejection of him, she had heightened the tension between them to an intolerable level, reinforced his shameful opinion of her, and shamed herself.

She felt physically and mentally drained as she crept downstairs, finding herself, without being aware of how she had got there, crouching in front of the fire. She could go; he would not stop her now. But she knew she couldn't take the coward's way.

That she would be exhausted before she had managed
to cover any helpful distance was beside the point. She
had to stay and face him again, because, in one blinding
moment of insight, she knew that walking out with
nothing resolved between them would bring a sense of
loss, a diminished self-respect, that would haunt her all
her life.

The cottage was deathly still when she woke in the grey
dawn light. The wind had dropped and the silence pressed
drearily on her and she moved stiffly, having fallen asleep
at last on the small sofa. She drew back the curtains to
a heavy, steel-grey morning then went to check on the
bird.

It was standing, its feathers ruffled, bright beady eyes
watching her warily, and she smiled. Its recovery was
one good thing, a heartening thing, and she let herself
into the kitchen where she made up some dried milk,
warmed it and added a few breadcrumbs to the saucer,
hoping to tempt the robin to eat; although she was sure
that bread and milk was hardly its proper diet, she could
but hope.

Running her bath, she tried to ignore the fluttery
feelings of apprehension that were beginning to make
her feel on edge, almost ill. Waldo's moods had been
chancy at the best of times, only rarely allowing the real
man to show through. But this morning, she guessed,
his mood would be diabolical. And in all honesty, she
couldn't blame him. So she had to talk to him, make
him understand what had happened, why she had rejected his lovemaking when he had been well aware of
how much she had wanted him. She needed, fiercely,
without knowing exactly why, to gain his trust, his
respect.

She could have done with a change of clothes, but
didn't feel up to intruding, scrabbling through her case
for something fresh to wear when he might wake at any
moment and tell her to get the hell out. So she made do
with the things she'd worn yesterday and slept in, and
trudged downstairs to put the kettle on. She felt twisted
up inside, but thinking about the dark tangle that was
her fraught relationship with Waldo wasn't going to help
her to achieve the degree of calmness that would be es-
sential if she were to try to hold a rational conversation
with him, convince him that she had not been responsible for Eden's death, that she was neither a gold-digger
nor a promiscuous tramp. This had become, for now,
the most important thing in her life. She didn't know
why it should be, but it was. In a way, she wished she
simply didn't care what he thought of her. It would be
so much easier to collect her things and walk out, without
a backward thought or look.

The bird had eaten some of the bread and milk—
Hannah could see traces clinging to the tiny beak—eaten
some and trodden on the rest, spilling it. She removed
the saucer and mopped up, replacing the wet tissues with
those she'd brought down with her. When she went to
fetch more logs she sniffed the slightly warmer air, heard
the drip of melting snow from the eaves and knew the
forecast thaw had not come a moment too soon.

The tea and toast made, she ate her own breakfast in
the kitchen. No sign of life from upstairs. So Waldo was
either still sleeping or refusing to face her. She didn't
think it was the latter. He would always face what had
to be faced.

The toast was proving difficult to swallow, so she left
it, every nerve-end stretched for any sound from him.
She assuredly wasn't looking forward to the embar-

rassment of seeing him, but, perversely, she wished he would start his day so that she could get the humiliating business of apologising, explaining, out of the way and behind her. And, with luck, she would gain his understanding, reverse his awful opinion of her, force him to see her with new eyes.

Eventually, as if to reassure herself that her day *could* continue without him, she busied herself outside, clearing the snow from the front of the cottage. It was quite slushy now, she noted with satisfaction, so her efforts were probably pointless. But it did give her something to do, stopped her from thinking about him.

Leaning on the shovel, her cheeks flushed from her exertions, she unbuttoned her jacket and wondered if he'd come downstairs yet. Then, annoyed with herself for allowing him to intrude into her mind yet again when the sole purpose of shovelling snow had been to put him out of it, she set out in the direction of the abandoned car, picking her way through the wet snow, using the tracks he'd made the day before.

Half-way across the sea of white she saw an approaching figure. A small old man wearing a sack over his shoulders, carrying two bottles of milk in mittened hands.

He had to look up to her and his old blue eyes held a knowing twinkle as he asked,

'You staying at Eyesore along with Waldo?'

She nodded. Eyesore? The name of the cottage? The old man grinned, pushing the milk into her hands.

'Picked two extra up from the milk van. Thought you could do with it. Waldo can see me right some other time. And tell him the lane's been cleared through to the end of his track. If he wants a hand digging through to the lane, I'm willing. Tell him Len's willing.' He had begun to turn, but he grinned gappily over his bent shoulders. 'But if I was in his shoes I wouldn't be in any hurry to leave!'

He went then, wallowing back through the snow, but not before his knowing old eyes had witnessed the colour that flooded her face. Hannah stared after his retreating figure, clutching the bottles of milk, feeling like the gauche teenager she'd been when Edward had begun his pursuit of her.

The embarrassed colour receded at last and she squared her shoulders. So what if the locals thought that Waldo Ross was having the time of his life, marooned in the cottage—Eyesore! That surely couldn't be its name!—with his woman of the moment. Nothing could be further from the truth!

But she almost dropped the bottles of milk as a fresh wave of agitation shook her. It very nearly had been the truth! There were shades of truth; she was beginning to see that now. Nothing was ever black and white.

She had discovered the truth about Eden, or thought she had. She had certainly taken it as being, not just one part of him, a side of his character she could never live with, but as the whole truth, the whole man. She had done her best to help him, to give him support and understanding, but he had resented her efforts, called her a mealy-mouthed parson's daughter, asked her where she kept her halo, told her to get out of his life if all she could do was sermonise. But perhaps if Eden had lived long enough, he could have been persuaded to accept help—not hers, necessarily, since he didn't seem able to forgive her for breaking off their engagement—then he might have changed, become the man she had previously believed him to be. She would never know now.

Suddenly, without knowing where the thought came from, or why it had come, she desperately needed to talk to Waldo about her relationship with Eden, its disturbing end. If he were ever to trust her—he *had* to trust her!—then he must be made to listen to the truth.

She turned, retracing her steps, sure he'd be down by now. But there was no sign of him and her shoulders slumped in unreasonable dejection. She'd been outside for the best part of two hours so he must have come down and gone out. Chopping more logs? Or just out, walking aimlessly in the snow because he couldn't stand the sight of her? That thought hurt.

Hannah fed the robin again, fresh milk this time with the breadcrumbs, then, her heart strangely heavy because she needed to see Waldo, talk to him, set things straight between them and he was avoiding her like the plague, she went upstairs to change her trousers which were damp to the knees where the slushy snow had come over the tops of her boots.

Pushing open the bedroom door, she saw that he hadn't even bothered to open the curtains, had left the bed unmade in an untidy heap. Flinging the curtains wide, she turned to rummage in her case and saw that the unmade bed still held his outstretched form.

Hannah grew very still and her pulses juddered as she picked up the harsh sound of his breathing. Something was wrong—very wrong, she amended as she approached the bed. His face was white, even whiter around the mouth, and sweat dewed his skin.

'Waldo?' She spoke urgently, her eyes on the fluttering dark lashes as they lifted heavily, his mouth twisting in a spasm of pain as he struggled to sit up.

'Are you ill?' An inane question, and it didn't get an answer, didn't deserve one because a two-year-old would have known there was something very wrong. And suddenly he jerked back the duvet and swung his feet to the floor. He was naked, his entire body glistening with sweat, the flesh rippling with fine tremors, and before she could do anything to help he was staggering to the bathroom and moments later she heard the sound of his retching.

Panicky anxiety for him sent her scampering in pursuit, her heart thudding. He was leaning against the wall, visibly shaking, and he told her hoarsely, 'Get out, dammit!'

Hannah ignored that. If he thought she was getting some kind of kick out of seeing him this vulnerable then he was way off the mark. His vulnerability went to her heart like a knife, opening it to a wave of tenderness that was a sharp, sweet pain. He was ill, and it wasn't in her to leave him to get on with it alone. She wanted to help him, comfort him, wanted it with a strength that surprised her, he was bringing out all that was tender and maternal in her, and that surprised her, too.

Reaching his bathrobe from the hook on the door, she held it out to him and, when he merely stared at it, his expression slightly puzzled, muzzy, as if he were trying to make out what it was and couldn't, she moved close enough to drape it round his shoulders, her cat-green eyes narrowing as her heart punched her ribs. He disturbed her; even shuddering and ill, he disturbed her deeply.

'Come back to bed,' she told him, appalled to find her voice emerging huskily, almost as hoarse as his, as if her words had a connotation far removed from the common sense, the cold reality, that had inspired them.

Steeling herself, she put out a helping hand, making brief contact with his elbow before the expected re-

jection as he shrugged it away, muttering tersely,
'Dammit, leave me alone, can't you? I don't want you
around me.'

Hannah stood in the bathroom after watching him
stagger out, clutching at the slipping bathrobe. He didn't
want her near him, and that wasn't surprising after what
had happened last night, and given his present con-
dition. He had any virile male's objection to being seen,
by a woman who had so recently rejected his sexual
overtures, in this debilitated vulnerable state. And his
loathing of her, of the type of woman he thought she
was, was just the right adhesive to make her presence
utterly intolerable.

But even though he didn't want her around he needed
her—though he would be the last person to admit it! She
would just have to grit her teeth and ignore his sniping,
discover what was wrong with him, if she could, try to
assess how serious it was.

Stiffening her shoulders, she descended the stairs,
made a pot of tea and took a cup up to him, her resolve
almost expiring as he growled irritably, 'Don't want it.
Get lost.'

As calmly as she could, Hannah put the cup down on
the bedside table. He was feverish, his dark hair clinging
wetly to his skull, his face white, dewed with sweat. His
body needed fluid. If she went downstairs, left him to
it for a short while, then maybe he would have the sense
to drink. But before leaving, she had to say,

'I think you ought to have a doctor. I'll go
now——'

'No. Don't need one.' His taut reply was implicit with
his desire to see the back of her and she left him, unhappy about it, but realising that, at the moment, her
presence was doing no good at all.

She heard him stagger to the bathroom three times in quick succession, heard the painful sound of his retching, the inevitable heavy, faltering footsteps as he returned to his room. It was cold up there, and he was ill, and it worried her so that she was edgy, jumpy like a cat.

After twenty endless minutes she could stand it no more and she filled a glass with water and went upstairs. No matter how he loathed the sight of her, she couldn't just leave him. Like it or not, he was going to have to let her look after him. If twenty-four hours ago anyone had told her that she would be worried half out of her mind because Waldo Ross had taken to his bed with some nameless illness, she would have laughed in their faces. But she wasn't laughing now.

The harsh rasp of his breathing intensified the silence of the room, the chill, the feeling of isolation. He seemed deeply asleep, but it didn't seem to be a healthy, re-storing sleep, and as she put her hand on his brow and felt its heat she knew she would have been running to phone a doctor had there been a phone in the house. But there wasn't and it could take her hours to contact one if she set out on foot. She didn't want to leave him alone for that long, but if she could persuade him to drink, pile extra blankets on him to keep him warm, she would set out to find the nearest house or phone box.

The cup of tea was still on the bedside table, quite cold now, and Hannah put the glass of water beside it. He would have to drink something; the fever was burning him up, he could be dehydrating.

Her movements calmer than her thoughts, she fetched a bowl of cold water and a face flannel from the bathroom, and gently began to bathe his face, his neck, his chest. His eyelids flickered briefly, a moan of protest coming from deep inside his throat, and she spoke to him, her voice deliberately calm and clear.

'Wake up, Waldo. You must drink something.'

He opened one eye and she hastily expunged her anxious frown, replacing it with an expression of unflappable severity.

'Can you sit up?'

'No.'

He looked so much like a truculent child that Hannah's heart flipped sweetly and she bit her lips to hide a smile. For a moment back there she had thought he was about to die on her and the relief was heady.

'Then I shall help you.' Her voice, her movements, were calculatedly brisk, impersonal, but there was nothing impersonal about the ungovernable flutter of excitement that juddered its way through her as she slid her hands beneath the breadth of his shoulders, his burning skin searing her palms with dizzying sensations. Nothing impersonal at all.

Sitting on the side of the bed, supporting his head with one arm, her fingers curling into his damp black hair, she took a steadying breath and reached for the glass of water. His eyes were regarding her with steady, black hostility, and she evaded them quickly. She would not let his obvious antagonism deflect her. She was made of sterner stuff and was going to help him even if he couldn't stand the sight of her. All she had to do was let him see who was boss.

But easier said than done. Hannah sucked in her breath as he demonstrated that, jerking his head aside as she held the water to his lips.

'I told you to leave me alone, woman!' His voice was a dry croak and he was weak and white around the lips, but he was still capable of knocking the glass from her hands and before she had time to take evasive action he did just that, his arms flailing petulantly.

Swallowing an unladylike oath, Hannah scrambled to her feet, impaling him with cross, narrowed eyes. She didn't notice the brief look of contrition, and something more—so brief it was gone like a forgotten fragment of a dream—and she ignored his, 'You look like a spitting cat,' his husky voice making the words sound incredibly sexy.

'Right!' There was an explosion building up inside her and her breasts were heaving, straining against the wet wool of her sweater, two spots of angry colour staining her cheeks. 'If you want to act like a spoiled brat, then go right ahead. I'll go right now and leave you to it. But if you want to get back on your feet again before the moon turns blue you're going to have to forget your stupid male pride, forget you think I'm poison, and do as I damned well tell you! It's up to you, buster!'

Whatever he said, she had no intention of leaving him like this, but he wasn't to know that; she hadn't known it herself until she'd got that load of rage off her chest. She stood perfectly still, catching her breath in the aftermath of that flash of blinding anger, watching for a sign from him, any sign. All she got was a surly grunt, which could have meant anything. But it was enough and she stumped across the room, still seething but nothing like as violently, and dragged a small mahogany-framed armchair to the side of the bed.

'Sit there while I change the sheets you've just soaked.' She didn't give him time to argue, just jerked the duvet off the bed, averting her eyes from his nudity, not offering to help as he crawled out, groaning. He didn't want her touching him and she didn't want to start another fight, but she tossed him the duvet before she went for fresh sheets.

She hurried, fetching the sheets from the airing cupboard in the bathroom, re-making the bed, tinglingly aware of the way he was watching her. It was cold in here and if she could have managed the large gas cylinder up the stairs she would have fetched the heater. As it was, she held out the robe he had kicked to the foot of the bed.

'Put this on. Then I'll fill a hot water bottle and go for a doctor.' She was talking to cover the awkwardness of the moments when he was struggling to get into the towelling robe, and as tying the belt seemed beyond him, she did it, feeling the heat of his body as she came closer.

There was a strange, poignant intimacy about this moment, almost painful, and she swallowed on the lump in her throat as she watched him roll back on to the bed, shaking with the series of tremors that shook him from time to time.

Covering him with the duvet she told him, 'You're going to have to drink something, you'll burn up if you don't.' She collected the sheets, the empty glass, and walked from the room, only then allowing her forehead to pucker with the anxiety she felt burning inside her as surely as the fever burned him.

There was a hot water bottle in a cupboard downstairs and she put the kettle on to heat, filling the glass with water again and searching through her flight bag for the aspirins she knew she had. Maybe they wouldn't do much good, but they wouldn't do any harm—if she could per-suade the brute to swallow them! But since her explosion of rage, and come to think of it her sweater was still wet with the water he'd knocked everywhere, he had appeared to be more docile.

A few minutes later she was trudging back upstairs, her apprehension affecting her so that her movements felt sluggish. If he decided to play up, act like a recalcitrant child again, there would be little she could do to help. Even ill he was far stronger than she. There was nothing weak at all about this man.

But he had decided to co-operate, apparently, making no objection when she slid the hot water bottle under the covers then held out the water, the two aspirins in the palm of her hand.

'If I'm sick again it will be your fault,' he told her grumpily, but without his previous rancour, and then collapsed back against the pillows, seemingly asleep.

The fever was responsible for the way he could so suddenly fall asleep. Taking advantage of his comatose state to get out of her wet sweater and the still-damp trousers she had meant to change earlier, she selected a soft skirt in indigo fine wool and a matching bloused top. Hardly suitable gear, even with her fur jacket, for the icy conditions she would experience while going to contact a doctor. After phoning, giving the doctor details of where Waldo was, she could also phone for a cab. There was nothing at all to stop her leaving. But the thought was dismissed immediately. No way could she leave him. She wanted to look after him; his vulnerability had brought out all that was tender and caring in her.

So she would phone for a doctor and get back here as fast as her legs would carry her and if she half froze in the process, well, so be it; she had run out of anything more suitable to wear.

Stripping down quickly after casting a glance at his sleeping figure, she stepped into fresh oyster lace briefs and was about to clip the fastening of the matching bra when his voice hit her, the shockwaves more intense for the lazy tone he used.

'You have a beautiful body. A pity to hide it. Come here.'

Hannah, beetroot-red, did no such thing. What a fool! She should have changed in the bathroom, not taken his attitude of deep sleep for granted. Hadn't she learned by now that this man was nothing if not completely unpredictable!

Jerkily, she scrambled into her clothes, shivering as much from the effect his words had had on her as from the chilly atmosphere. She had thought the wretch was asleep, half dead, and all the time he must have been watching her every movement—as if she'd been staging a striptease to help his convalescence along! And it was a total turn-around for him. Maybe the fever had mushed his brain, it was the only answer she could come up with.

She would have gone then. She felt in dire need of a stiff medicinal dose of his whisky to warm her before she faced the snow outside, but his voice, the rasping quality of it, stopped her.

'Hannah—I'm sorry.'

And that, coming from him, was one big concession. She wasn't going to delve more deeply, ask what, in particular, he was sorry about. She could list a hundred things he could be apologising for! Instead, she said loftily, 'That's perfectly all right. Can I get you anything before I go? A cup of tea? Something to eat?'

He shuddered at that last offhand suggestion but his dark eyes held her, their unprecedented softness softening something in her, 'I could murder a cup of tea.'

'Coming up.' Oh, how severe, cool, she sounded, she thought wryly, closing the door quietly behind her. And how very very clever to keep her tumultuous thoughts from surfacing. He only had to look at her, his eyes melting, and she forgot the indignities he had heaped upon her, the insults he'd hurled at her, and became jelly-like, a quivering mass of contradictory female instincts, eager to do his slightest bidding, to care for him to the best of her ability, to face the arctic conditions out there in order to bring qualified help to him. She had never imagined she could be such a fool.

She put the tea things on a tray, taking an extra cup for herself because she could do with a hot drink, and she approached the side of the bed, her manner brisk and breezy, feeling that Florence Nightingale herself would have been proud of the way she was handling the situation.

'Here we are then, tea, as ordered!' Her voice had a ghastly chirpiness about it that would have made her cringe in any other circumstances. But this bright, falsely hectoring tone suited the occasion, she was sure it did. To show him how desperately anxious she was, how his vulnerability softened her, got to her in a way she hadn't imagined possible in regard to him, would be unthinkable.

She made room for the tray on the bedside table, flicking on the lamp because the winter afternoon was drawing to a close, darkening the room. And she poured two cups and passed him his.

'Can you manage?' She didn't look at him as he struggled to sit up against the pillow; he would have caught the unstoppable look of compassion in her eyes. But she saw the outstretched shaking hand as he reached for the cup, the way he sagged back against the pillows, his eyes closing, the thick sweep of dark lashes a startling contrast against the pallor of his skin.

'Help me?' The plea seemed torn from him, against his will, and she knew he had to be feeling like death to have brought himself to ask for assistance from her.

Swallowing against the tightness in her throat, the gathering of stupid tears, she sat on the edge of the bed, supporting his head with her arm, holding the cup to his lips. His head felt heavy, but its weight was a load she gladly bore, and that knowledge, coming suddenly, shook her.

Her fingers tightened involuntarily against the hot dry skin of his shoulder and she wondered if, by some strange alchemy, that thought had been transmitted to him because he shook his head after one or two sips, his eyes searching hers.

'Hold me. I'm cold. So cold.'

She couldn't have denied him even if she'd wanted to. And she didn't want to. She *needed* to hold him, comfort him. With unsteady hands she put the cup back on the tray then slid beneath the covers beside him, her arms wound round his body, the length of her pressed to the length of him. And he was cold.

Involuntary spasms racked his hard frame and his mouth was clenched in a rictus of pain; as soon as he seemed easier she was going to run for her life to find a doctor.

Carefully, Hannah inched further up the bed, the better to support him, and he turned his head to her breasts, burrowing into her softness as she held him, her other hand slipping under the towelling robe, gently massaging the tense muscles of his shoulders, finding the knotted cords at the nape of his neck.

Beneath her fingers his skin felt like burning silk, the aching shudders still rippling through him, but he began to relax, at last, as her soothing hands released the knotted tension. It was then, as he pressed his face more deeply into the warmth of her body, that she realised that her breathing was as raggedly irregular as his. And worse than that, far worse, she longed with a primitive, savage need to open the buttons of the top she wore to allow him access to her naked flesh.

The need confused her, short-circuited the orderly currents of her brain. She didn't know what was happening to her. She felt disorientated, pushed out of orbit. She only knew that this man had spelled trouble from the beginning and, after last night, she ought to have been able to squash such untenable longings.

Trying to bring order to the chaos of her mind she said, her voice holding only a trace of a tremor, 'It's thawing well now. I'll have no trouble getting a doctor out to you. I'll be back as soon as I can.'

'No.' His husky voice was muffled as he snuggled closer to her, his arms holding her. 'Don't leave me.'

Her breath held for one long, incredulous moment. He was in no fit state to consider the possibility of her defection, his need to confront her with Lottie, and that surmise sent crazy shivers of delight through her until she regained enough sanity to remember how ill he was. He probably didn't know, or care, who she was; she was merely a nameless female body he could snuggle close to, like a child. He didn't want her, in particular, to stay with him, hold him, help him through his illness.

Using two fingers beneath his chin she tipped his head back, away from her breasts which had, shamingly, hardened with an almost intolerable need, and a wry smile tugged the corners of her mouth as she saw how her action had brought a cross pucker to his brow. But she held him away from her, waiting for his eyes to open, and, when they did—thwarted slits of jet—she had to

bite her lips to stop her laughter, to stop the kiss she
yearned to put on his sulky mouth.

'Waldo, I have to go now. To contact a doctor.'

'I don't need one,' he muttered crossly, trying to bury
his head in her breast again. But her fingers had developed a tensile strength from somewhere, the tips of
them discovering his hard jawline beneath the dark, incipient beard.

'You need medication,' she admonished as sternly as
she could. 'Any fool could see that.'

'No.' He stared at her blackly. 'I've been through this
before, it's some type of jungle fever.' It seemed too
much effort for him to talk now, but he carried doggedly
on, with the determination that was such a strong part
of his character. 'Picked up the bug several years ago
out east. It recurs, like malaria. Affects me less each
time, though.' He passed his tongue over parched lips.
'A couple of days—I'll be fine. Back to normal, believe
me.'

She would have to, wouldn't she? And when he commanded huskily, 'Just hold me,' she had to do that, too.
If he was right—and there was no reason why he should
lie to her—and this was a recurring tropical fever, then
he would be all right. It was frightening, but not
dangerous. She recalled enough from the first aid and
home nursing course she had taken, at her mother's
behest, to feel confident of giving him all the care he
needed.

Trailing her fingers along the line of stubble, she
allowed his head to turn again to her breast where he
relaxed, limp and contented, and she settled herself more
comfortably, her fingers softly kneading the nape of his
neck as his body quietened, dropping into sleep.

As she watched him, he seemed heart-wrenchingly vulnerable, his face hollowed, his mouth less harsh, and this new aspect of him touched her deeply. A fresh emotion was born, expanding her, strengthening her love for him in the desire to cherish, a desire that had been with her since she had found him ill, and one that she had not truly recognised until now.

Her *love* for him! As the import of her wandering thoughts penetrated her mind more deeply, Hannah's body became rigid. She totally rejected it. The thought had sprung from nowhere—surely it had?

There had always been this intense awareness of him, of his voice, of his glance, his lightest touch. And last night that tingling awareness had grown, exploding into a violent physical need that had been in direct opposition to what she knew of herself. It had been a strong physical desire, no more than that. And her need to cherish was quite ordinary, really, simply the natural re-action of a caring person to someone suddenly stricken. She had to be weak in the head to even imagine herself in love with him!

Appalled, she tried to ease herself off the bed, but her first tentative movement away from him brought his arms tightening around her, his body half on top of her, pinning her down, and she subsided weakly, unaccus-tomed tears trickling beneath her closed eyelids as her body's instinctive reaction to his sent sensation after sensation coursing through her.

Eventually he slept, but Hannah could not move; if she tried to leave him he would wake. The weight of his head nestled beneath her chin, the arm he had curved around her, the pinioning leg, were like a drug. She didn't want to move, not now. His sleeping body transmitted sensations entirely new to her, an amalgam of erotic excitement, a sadness-tinged yearning that made her want to cry because, despite the frantic denials of her mind, she knew she loved him.

Despite what her intellect had tried to tell her, her body had been truthful and she acknowledged that now. The time for self-deception had gone. Never promiscuous, her body had instinctively responded to his, recognising its mate. And now her mind accepted him, too, accepted the fact of the birth of love.

Tenderly, her fingers idled over the hard planes and angles of his face, lingering at the corner of the mobile male mouth. Physically, he had dominated her by forcing her here, and, on another plane, he had exercised his effortless domination over her senses, her heart, her soul. She had fallen in love with a man who loathed and despised her, and she had never done anything so damn stupid in her life!

# CHAPTER SEVEN

HANNAH, my girl, she told herself mutely as, at some time during the night, he cuddled more closely to her, almost covering her with his body, you are in a whole load of trouble.

She hadn't slept, hadn't wanted to. Every second had to be savoured, bittersweet, to be held on to. Because when he was himself again he wouldn't want to know her, much less hold her, take comfort from her warm woman's body. So tonight was time stolen and she, the thief of time, would have these finite moments, minutes, hours, to keep for ever and he would never know she had taken them.

In the darkness, not seeing the darkness, her wide-awake eyes saw instead every searching look he had ever given her, the subtle and the not-so-subtle nuances of expression, every mannerism, the elegant yet faintly arrogant way he held his body, moved, the way his mouth felt against hers, the touch of his hand, the scent of him when the cold night air clung, the elusive golden lights in wicked black eyes...

Hannah woke, annoyed that she had slept at all, wasted precious moments when she could have pretended that her love for him was not the pointless thing it was, when his arms, holding her, could have been the arms of one who loved in return.

Waldo was beginning to surface from sleep, murmuring, his hands moving, unerringly finding the place where his head had rested through the night, finding the swelling softness, the twin source of comfort, demanding more than comfort now as slowly, with a gentleness that took her breath away, his fingers moulded the too-willing flesh, the erotic movements arousing the tightened peaks. She felt his maleness dominate her, inflame her senses like a potent drug, and she bit on her lips in an agony of wanting, of knowing she had no right to the sensations he was provoking.

Her protest was unambiguous, but almost silent, merely a muted whimpering as she took his hands in hers, drawing them away from her breasts, denying herself the touch that reduced her to a craving creature, a victim of her own hammering senses, her own pointless needs.

She rolled out of the bed, careless of the fact that she was bringing him fully awake. He had only done what any man would have done, only half awake, maybe even feverish still, with a warm woman's body in his arms. That he should at last come fully awake, discover that he was caressing a woman he had admitted he loathed, and that she, not only allowing the intimacy, was actively revelling in it, would be too shamingly hurtful to hear!

'Hannah?' The black eyes were still unfocused, hazed with sleep, with dreams perhaps, and her heart turned over with love for him as she straightened her crumpled clothing, collected the long-forgotten tea tray, smiling a big bright smile that didn't touch her eyes because her eyes were looking inward, seeing their inevitable parting, the emotional emptiness of the years ahead, and he would not, must not, know about that. She had been the fool who had blindly fallen in love.

'Feeling better?' Oh, the brightly impersonal enquiry—she should have gone on the stage!

'Much, thanks. What are you doing?'

'A hundred and one things.' Again the pasted smile, the quick bright look, the look that lied because the truth was in the shaking of her hands, the tight hard lump that constricted her throat.

'But aren't you going to look after me? I'm a sick man.' He was teasing her from the depths of the big bed, the light in his eyes devilish, and he looked totally better.

She said, sweetly tart, 'At least a hundred of those hundred and one are down to you,' and swept out on what she considered to be a good exit line.

Hannah felt tacky but she only made time for a quick wash, for cleaning her teeth. Miraculously, the snow was diminished to a shrunken greyish slush. The sitting-room fire was out, but that was predictable, and the robin was out, too, perching on the back of the sofa, evading her hands when she tried to catch it. She said softly, conceding defeat, 'Time to go?' but she was going to have to leave that until later, until she'd warmed some milk for Waldo. So she put crumbs on a tray, a dish of water, and left the bird to forage for itself.

Back in the kitchen she could hear Waldo moving overhead, in the bathroom, running water, and she called up the stairs, 'Are you all right? I'll bring you a hot drink up.'

He shouted back, 'I'm coming down,' and that threw her into a flurry of thwarted domesticity.

If there had been any fresh eggs in the place she would have scrambled some. But there weren't. A hasty rummage in the freezer brought kippers to light, the boil-in-the-bag variety. She lit the gas heater, put a pan of

water on the hotplate and the kettle to boil for tea, too
concerned with scurrying around, worrying whether he
was fit enough to leave his bed, and knowing there wasn't
a thing she could do about it if he weren't because he
was a man who made his own mind up, to hear his tread
on the stairs.

He was freshly shaved, his hair still wet from the
shower, dressed in fawn hip-hugging cords, a heavy fawn
sweater. He still looked pale, his face gaunt—but better,
much better.

Leaning against the wall at the foot of the stairs, he
gave her a long, complicated look that had her colour-
ing with confusion. He had always confused her, but
now doubly so, her own knowledge of her deep feelings
for him adding to the turmoil. She felt weak with love
for him, and the way she felt was a problem she didn't
know how to tackle, not yet. She needed time to get her
thoughts into some kind of coherent order, and right
now there was no time because he was crowding her.

Swinging away, her jet hair forming a curtain to hide
behind, she babbled, 'I don't know how your appetite
is, but I'm cooking kippers. But if you'd prefer toast
and tea—or warm milk—no problem. I'm——'

'Kippers and tea will be fine.' He cut across her
breathless torrent, his voice amused, but a thread of
tension still there which she, with her heightened sen-
sitivity to everything about him, picked up. So much
had happened since they'd almost made love. She remembered his anger—she didn't think she'd ever forget
it—remembered his hating, and wondered if he was remembering, too.

But he said, his voice a seduction in itself, 'I like your
hair that way.'

Loose, her thick, dark hair was inclined to curl with a turbulent beauty that was unique to her. She made her hands busy with plates, cutlery, tried to ignore the hot run of pleasure his unlooked-for compliment gave her.

'I didn't make time to braid it this morning.'

But she knew he had seen through her attempt at non-chalance because of the odd tight smile that lifted one corner of his mouth as he said, 'I wonder.'

Did he guess the way she felt about him? Surely not, her heart hammered a frantic denial. He couldn't. He mustn't—not now, not until things had been resolved between them. And even then, he still probably wouldn't want to know.

The way she would set about resolving the problems between them was something she was going to have to think long and hard about. She poured the tea, divided the kippers on to two plates and told him to sit down before he fell.

'Fresh milk?' One dark eyebrow lifted, questioning the bottle she'd brought out of the fridge, and she explained, glad to get on to safe territory.

'An old man brought it, said his name was Len, said you could see him right some other time. He also told me that the lane at the end of the track is clear.' She didn't add that he'd offered to help dig Waldo's car out, clear the track. He wouldn't be up to such strenuous physical exercise for some days and although she guessed she and Len could do it, and that she wouldn't put up a showing she'd need to be ashamed of, she didn't want to leave just yet. They could wait until the thaw did the job for them, and she'd be quite happy if it took weeks! Strange how love drove common sense out of sight——
She needed time if she were to ever come to terms with the way she felt about him, to discover, if she could, if

there was the remotest chance that he might see her as she was, and not as he believed her to be.

Feeling his eyes on her, on the changing expressions that flickered across her features, she gabbled on, 'Len called this place "Eyesore". Surely you didn't pick that as a name? It's anything but!'

He was toying with his fish, pushing it around his plate. He looked suddenly weary, but he smiled at her show of indignation.

'Officially, it's Marsh End Cottage—there's a mile and a half of salt marsh between here and the sea—but before I bought it, had it renovated, it had been lived in for thirty years by a family who'd never done a thing to it except tack on rusty corrugated iron lean-tos. The locals got used to calling it Eyesore, and the name stuck.'

'Oh, I see.' She finished the fish which had been delicious. 'And you don't live here all the time—obviously not. Are you based mainly abroad?'

She was prying, she knew she was, but it seemed desperately important to know as much about him as he could be prevailed upon to tell her. The more he told her, the more there would be to remember.

'Mostly,' he answered lightly. 'But lately I've been spending more time in the UK. I've a flat in London,' he shrugged expressively, 'but it's not a home. Recently, I've been thinking of putting down roots, delegating more, so I'm seriously considering buying a house.'

'Oh.' It was all she could say. From what she knew of him, of his globe-wandering past, the way Lottie had said he was a little on the wild side, his desire to put down roots had come as a surprise. But then he'd been full of surprises all along the line.

She gathered her wits together and asked brightly, taking an interest, 'Where? London?'

'No way. I need to breathe,' he added succinctly, then tacked on, surprising her again with the wounding intent behind the words, 'No doubt you would die of boredom away from the bright lights, the glamour.'

'I can't think why you should say that.' She could, but she wasn't going to admit it. Surely now was the time to tell him the truth about her relationship with Eden, but somehow she couldn't do it. Not yet. Not now. The truth about Eden would hurt him dreadfully, and she couldn't bring herself to inflict that kind of pain, not while he was still weak from the fever. He had obviously not known what was happening to his brother; he had been out of the country for so long. She hadn't known, either, until two months before the date set for their wedding—and she had been Eden's fiancée!

Gathering her empty plate and cup, she stood up, the fine tremors of her hands showing how much his gibe had hurt. 'I was brought up in a country vicarage,' she told him, her voice tight with pain. 'I spent my early years climbing trees, fishing, finding the snares the farmers had set for rabbits and foxes and pulling them out and burying them at the bottom of our garden— when I wasn't helping Mother with the Sunday school or Father around the parish.'

And no doubt you imagined I spent my formative years in shady back-street city dives, she added mentally, acidly, frowning as she turned back to the table and found his eyes on her in a long, questioning look that did nothing for her equilibrium. She wished he wouldn't look at her that way, as if he disbelieved every word she said. The feeling was stark, painful, and she wanted him to trust her, believe in her, more than she had ever wanted anything. But to gain that trust she would have to shatter his memories of Eden, tell him things that would hurt him, and she loved him too much to want to give him that kind of pain.

It was a problem she didn't know how to resolve. She raised her eyes to his, thrown off balance by the sheer male beauty of the hard-boned face, the indolent sex appeal of the tautly muscled lean body, and to cover the bittersweet anguish she snapped waspishly, 'If you don't eat you'll never get your strength back!' sounding so like her memory of her crabby maternal grandmother that she almost smiled.

But it was Waldo who did the smiling, tugging his dark forelock, 'Yes, ma'am.' He pushed himself to his feet and tipped his barely touched meal into the pedal bin. 'Take it gradually—I'll eat more this evening, ma'am, dear, and by the look of things,' more soberly now as he paused by the window, looking out, 'we ought to be able to get out of here tomorrow.'

Hannah tried to look pleased about that, but she couldn't. She had hoped for more time, much more time, because there was no way she was going to come up with a solution to the problem of telling him about Eden, altering his opinion of her, in the space of a few hours.

Leaving him to cope with the washing-up, she went to the sitting-room before he got the opportunity to see the weak tears that filled her eyes, to guess at the reason for them. She was behaving like an infatuated teenager, and she had to stop it.

The robin had found a perch in the nook over the broad beam that straddled the hearth, and she talked to it for a while, getting hold of herself. Apart from that one gibe, Waldo had given no indication of how much he despised her. But she'd be living in a fool's paradise if she allowed herself to believe he'd forgotten precisely why he loathed her. He was suffering from the aftermath of fever, not amnesia! But if she could, somehow, make him believe in her, trust her, without her having to spell out how Eden had been, then her problem would be solved. It was a tall order, and she didn't see how it could be accomplished, but she'd work on it.

Lighting the fire gave her something to do; besides, they could hardly sit in the kitchen all day. And it would be a long day, she knew that, both dreading and welcoming the hours of enforced proximity.

She was an emotional mess, and there seemed little to be done about it, not now, not when the memory of how near they had been to making love, of how she had felt when she had cradled him in her arms through the night, was so immediate, so vivid.

She loved him, despite what he had done in bringing her here against her will, despite the way he thought of her. Unlike her feelings for Eden, which had been lukewarm at best, then utterly repelled by what she had come to know of him, she knew she would love Waldo until her dying gasp, no matter what he did. She had to be weak in the head!

Stirring herself, knowing she had to face him, act normally, figure out a way of persuading him to believe she was not the voracious man-eating monster he entrenchedly believed her to be, without telling him the complete and hurtful truth about the brother he had loved—a tall order indeed—she marched determinedly to the kitchen. The blank, give-away-nothing expression on her face was immediately replaced by one of concern as Waldo appeared from outside, his arms piled with logs.

He looked grey with fatigue and her anxiety was vented in an irritable, 'For pity's sake, I could have done that!'

She followed him back into the room she had just left
and he smiled wearily.

'Stop clucking like a mother hen. I'm a big boy now.'

Too big, she thought defeatedly, as he tipped the logs
on to the hearth. Too stubborn, too sure of himself, and
far too male.

'Well, since you're so capable, big boy,' she chal-
lenged, 'suppose you catch that robin and let it out. It
can fend for itself now.'

'Sure it can.' Dark eyes followed the direction of her
pointing finger and he grinned. 'No problem.' And to
her immense chagrin, because she would have liked to
see him fail at something, but might have known he
wouldn't, he reached confident hands to the bird and
brought it down from its perch, the strong hands seeming
impossibly gentle.

'Like me, he's made a rapid recovery. We guys are
tough.' The man and the bird eyed each other with
mutual and sickening masculine self-congratulation and
Hannah snorted.

'That's only because the female around here looked
after you both!'

'So you did.' Black eyes lifted from smiling contemplation of the bird cupped in his capable hands and
the smile faded, leaving behind a look that pierced
Hannah's soul with sweetness. 'So you did.'

Turning quickly, before he could see her confusion,
she led the way from the room and she was beside him
as he released the bird, watching its flight to freedom.
She would have gone back inside but his hand, heavy
on her shoulder, twisted her round to face him.

'You could have gone, too, Hannah.' The line of his
mouth was taut, a faint questioning shadow in his eyes.
'It's obviously been thawing for some time. Less than a

mile would have brought you to the lane and the nearest farm. You could have phoned for a cab to take you to the nearest station. So why didn't you go, Hannah?'

She shrugged, trying to turn away, get back inside; anything was preferable to this dark scrutiny. There was no answer to his question except the truth and she wasn't ready to tell him that. Her decision to stay had been motivated by her strong desire to look after him, to resolve their quarrel, the anger that had sprung from that, the emotion that had almost torn them to pieces. And all that had been rooted in love—for her it was. She hadn't realised it at the time, but she did now.

'Instead,' he replied softly, ignoring the way she had refused to answer his question, his hands moving upwards, following the long pure line of her throat, 'you stayed, even though I told you to get out of my sight. You stayed and you fought me every inch of the way until I wanted nothing more than your presence, your nearness, your arms around me, holding me. Sometimes, I can't read you at all.'

With both hands he pushed the long hair back from her face, his hard fingers keeping her immobile. Hannah, trembling inside, met his eyes and the look she saw there made the blood thud heavily through her veins, her bones turn to jelly.

She knew he was going to kiss her and, weakly, she recognised that whatever else he wanted from her was his, because she knew she loved him now, would always love him; perhaps this was all she would ever have of him and perhaps it would be enough. It might have to be enough.

His kiss was perfection, as she had known it would be. The aggression, the almost primitive force she had felt in him before, had gone, and she gave herself to the sheer magic of it, her entire being concentrated on the intoxicating gentleness of his mouth on hers, the sensitive yet erotic probing of his tongue, its meeting with her own, the warm hands that held her still, so that he could take and taste and take again.

Slowly, with no guidance from her will because that was lost, her arms lifted, her hands seeking his nape, her body arching with female abandon to his, feeling the heady excitement as his hard male loins ground against hers, gently, so gently, the sensual circling movement setting her body on fire.

He wanted her, she was left in no doubt about that, and she loved him, and if she could make him believe in her integrity, just a little, then that would be a great step forward, and their coming together would have a deeper meaning for both of them.

'Waldo,' she murmured throatily, 'I want you to try to trust me. I never meant to hurt Eden—the whole thing was just impossible. Won't you believe me?'

Her whispering mouth moved against his, willing him to have faith in her, but she felt his body go still, rigid, and moved her head to meet his eyes.

'Waldo?' Her voice was a husky plea, and she saw the sudden flare of disgust in his eyes, impaling her. She sucked in her breath on a sob, half pain, half grief, his rejection a body blow. She had gambled and lost.

For long empty moments she stood where he'd left her, gathering enough strength to follow him inside. All he felt for her was lust; he would never believe she wasn't a tramp. And one word from her had been enough to remind him of the way the tramp had harmed his brother.

Her arms wrapped tightly around her body, as if to contain the pain that raged inside her, she followed him inside and found him making coffee. His curt words,

'Get your things together, we're leaving,' told her all she needed to know. He despised himself for desiring the tramp who had hurt his brother, and all he wanted now was to see the back of her.

She stumbled woodenly up the stairs. If he saw her misery he would put it down to the frustration of a vain woman, one who was used to calling the sexual tune. Well, so be it, she thought wretchedly, packing her case haphazardly, uncaring, tears falling unchecked, her agony almost beyond bearing.

The pain she had felt when Edward had told her he was married had been nothing compared to this. She could make him listen to the truth about Eden but it would only achieve more pain—pain for him if he believed her. And if her tentative mention of his brother, only minutes ago, and his reaction to it, was anything to go by, he wouldn't believe a word she said.

The only way forward for her was to build an impenetrable wall between them—so thick, so well founded, that neither of them would be able to breach it. It would be a bleak way, but it was the only way.

# CHAPTER EIGHT

'So YOU didn't go!' Gerald came to perch on the edge of her desk, his light brown eyes round with surprise. 'I don't believe I'm hearing this.'

But one look at the pale purity of her set features, the pallor of her skin—heightened by the midnight darkness of her hair—would have been enough to tell anyone that the last thing she'd been doing during the last three weeks was enjoying a winter holiday on the Atlas ski slopes under the north African sun.

Hannah shifted the pile of letters on her desk, her smile strained, and Gerald shook his head. 'So what did you do? Why didn't you get in touch? We could have spent a night or two on the tiles.'

Thankfully, she didn't have to answer that as Joyce, the communal secretary, came in with a package and Gerald slid off her desk shrugging, 'I'm going to lunch.'

'I don't know what you want doing about this.' Joyce put the bulky package on the top of the desk. 'I came across it just now and it reminded me. It's Eden Wilmott's book, poor boy.'

The unfinished manuscript had been with Hannah for yet another appraisal when the news of his death had come, and Hannah, with Roger's approval, had hung on to it for the time being. Returning it to his parents would have been rubbing salt in the wound. But it would have to go to them some time, maybe now?

Hannah rubbed the back of her neck tiredly and Joyce, who liked nothing better than a chat, sat down at

Gerald's empty desk. Joyce was plain, well into middle age and had been with Roger forever. She lived alone in a dreary little flat and took company where she could find it. Running her fingers through the back of her short iron-grey hair, she told Hannah, 'I met Eden's foster brother, you know, Waldo Ross I think it was—yes, Ross. Such a charming man——'

'You met Waldo?' Hannah's slanting green eyes narrowed.

Joyce preened, 'Oh, yes, he was so kind.' She leant back in the chair, obviously settled for the duration. 'I was leaving the office, a month or so after that terrible accident, and I slipped on the step—dropped my bag, my shopping. So embarrassing! But this really super chap picked everything up, including me, and insisted on taking me for a drink. He gave me brandy, for the shock, he said. Anyway,' Joyce was well in her stride now, 'it turned out he was Eden's foster brother—such a co-incidence, wasn't it?'

Hannah nodded absently, her pulses accelerating. Co-incidence, my foot! He had been investigating her and Joyce, ever willing to gossip indiscriminately, would have given him answers. But what answers?

'Naturally, I told him how sorry we all were about poor Eden, so tragic, especially so soon before you were to have been married. I didn't know, you hadn't said——' her hazel eyes accused briefly '—that you'd broken the engagement. Mr Ross told me that, asked how you'd taken the news, how you were bearing up now. So I told him you'd been shocked, like the rest of us, but not to worry, I said—he did look concerned in a way—you and Mr Gerald were seeing each other— he'd not long come back from the States then—and I could smell romance in the air!' She folded her hands over her plump stomach, her tongue working overtime, and Hannah thought, So he must have got a large amount of information from Joyce, who was so starved of company that she would tell her life story, and anyone else's, to any passing stranger.

'You've seen Waldo since?' she asked stonily, and Joyce nodded enthusiastically.

'Once or twice, when he happened to be passing as I was leaving,' and Hannah knew just how he had learned when she was taking her holiday, where she was going and at what time the cab was picking her up. She could have strangled Joyce on the spot!

'Coming across the manuscript reminded me,' Joyce told her, adding, 'Why don't we have lunch? You can tell me all about your holiday. I must say, though, it doesn't seem to have done you much good. You look as tired as you did before you went.'

'Sorry.' Hannah managed a suitably regretful smile. Joyce was a hopeless gossip, but there was no viciousness behind it, only loneliness. 'I've got masses of work to get through.'

The last thing Hannah wanted was the third degree from Joyce. It had been bad enough trying to fob Manda off. Manda rented the entire mews cottage next to the one where Hannah owned her flat. She was much in demand as a photographic model, but she made time to keep her friendship with Hannah alive. And she, putting it mildly, had been eaten up with curiosity when she had been sailing forth to one of her seemingly endless parties and had practically bumped into Hannah as Waldo had been lifting her case from the boot of his car.

Hannah didn't see Joyce leave the office; her thoughts were with Waldo again, as they so often were. The journey back from the cottage had been a nightmare, the roads still far from safe in places. Waldo hadn't looked fit to drive, but had curtly refused when Hannah had offered to take the wheel. His mood during the entire journey had been one of bitter withdrawal, his profile—whenever she'd risked a sideways look—grim. He hadn't spoken and neither had she, too choked up with pain to find any words, except when he'd finally pulled the car to a halt in front of her door and she'd said, 'Waldo, I——' But he'd cut her off, leaving the car abruptly, his face white and shuttered.

So she had scrambled out, fumbling miserably in her bag for her door key and Manda, stunning in a long white wool coat, her water-straight Titian hair falling to her shoulders, had emerged from her own door, raising arched brows above brown eyes.

'You're not back for another two weeks. So what——' The chirpy words had been cut off in mid-spate, the scarlet mouth forming a silent whistle, one eyelid closing in a knowing wink as Waldo, carrying Hannah's case, emerged from behind the sleek, dark car.

'Enough said! See you, sweetie!' Manda glided away, past the big, weary man, her sideways look openly appraising, and Hannah, feeling the strain the journey had put on him as if it were her own, offered—in spite of her earlier determination to build that wall—'Won't you come inside, relax, just while I fix you a drink, something to eat?'

'No.' The eyes that met hers were black and cold, his harsh features blank, and he dumped her case at her feet. She couldn't just let him go, not like this, fool that she was. 'Waldo, about Lottie——'

For a moment he looked as if he didn't know what she was talking about. And then he shrugged, already turning away. 'I still think it would be a good idea if you saw her. I'll be in touch.'

But he hadn't been in touch. For the remainder of her holiday Hannah had brooded around her flat, going out only when she needed to buy food supplies. She despised herself for being so spineless, for hanging around for a phone call from a man who had let her know, in no uncertain manner, that he loathed her. But she couldn't seem to talk any sense into herself.

He had been so adamant about taking her to see Lottie. He had even gone to the extent of abducting her, and no one could get more adamant than that, could they? He was a man who lived by his own absolute rules, always, and he took what he wanted—by force, if necessary. He faced the world alone, beholden to no one, only to his own sense of himself. Wise in the ways of the world, he was strong, the complete self-contained male, the hunter, the taker. So why hadn't he contacted her? Demanded that she go with him to face Lottie? For him to have given up on something he had been so determined to do was completely out of character.

She thought she could understand why they hadn't gone on to Great Yarmouth from the cottage. He had been ill, not over the fever—though he wouldn't have admitted that. She doubted if he had felt up to the confrontation he had spoken of, or the questions his foster father would have inevitably put. But to have simply abandoned his need to make her face up to what she was supposed to have done to Lottie? It didn't seem credible.

Hannah was certain of nothing, except that it would be a long time before she was free of him, even if the bondage lay only in her own mind and heart, in her captured senses.

And now, back at work, she hoped that would take her thoughts from him. But it didn't, and by mid week she was edgy enough to draw Roger's attention to her tension. And Gerald's sulks, because she consistently refused to see him out of office hours, added to the general depression of her days. It was time, she decided, to do something positive...

'Shall you be needing the car this weekend?'

'No. You want it, you take it, any time. Come in, don't stand on the doorstep like a purveyor of pegs.' Manda smiled widely, stepping aside and making an 'after you' gesture, and Hannah, feeling the cold wind tug at her skirts, her hair, shivered.

'Sorry, must dash.'

'Don't give me that!' Manda reached out and dragged her over the doorstep. 'You've been avoiding me for weeks, so you can spare me ten minutes now. If you want to borrow my motor you can give me some of your time.' Her low, throaty laughter took any sting out of her words and Hannah gave in; the last thing she wanted to do was snub her friend.

She followed the tall caftan-clad figure into the long sitting-room that ran the depth of the house, quietly dreading the questions she knew she would have to face, and Manda said, 'Find a pew, I'll fetch some wine.' Hannah sank on to a Victorian sofa, upholstered in rich velvet the colour of honeysuckle, and forced herself to relax, to respond to the elegant atmosphere.

'Here we are, sweetie,' Manda cooed, sweeping back in, the rich brocade of her caftan catching the light, echoing her Titian hair. 'Jeremy said this was an amusing little wine, so let's you and me have a real good giggle.'

She poured pale amber wine into tall cut crystal glasses and Hannah grinned for the first time in weeks. Manda was an incorrigible extrovert, larger than life; her beauty and personality attracting would-be lovers by the score. She accepted gifts from the richer of them, as if such homage were her due, and managed to keep them all at arms' length. Hannah didn't know how she did it.

'Mmm, nice.' Manda sipped the wine. 'He sent me a dozen bottles, so we can get pie-eyed if we like. Now, drink up and tell auntie all.' She sank crosslegged on to a Chinese rug, close to a bower of white jasmine in an oriental-style planter, and regarded Hannah with brown eyes that saw too much. 'You *are* looking fragile, dear thing. Anything to do with that beautiful man you brought home with you when, according to you, you should have been virtuously enjoying sport of the more outdoor kind in Marrakesh?'

Hannah had grown fond of Manda in the short time she'd known her and knew that the bubbly, breathless personality was mostly on the surface. Underneath, she was kind, discreet and caring, and Hannah knew she could unburden herself without any risk of anything going any further.

Twisting the wine glass in her hands, she told the facts of those traumatic days at the cottage, bluntly, baldly, not realising the impact of her words until Manda gave a long expressive whistle.

'My God, it's like something out of fiction. I can see why you fell for him, he's gorgeous! So what are you going to do about it?'

'Nothing.' Hannah sipped at her wine abstractedly, feeling it slip down her throat like silky sunlight, and she lifted her shoulders slightly, staring into the remaining honey-pale liquid. 'It's all crazy, like a dream, and I'm doing my best to put him out of my mind, but the devil won't go! So I'll go to see Lottie on Saturday, I have to do that, and afterwards—well, I shall forget it ever happened.' She pushed long strands of thick dark hair behind her ears, her eyes embarrassed, haunted, and Manda snorted.

'That's not the Hannah Sloane I've grown to know and admire! You want the guy, you go out and get him. Where's all that spunky spirit gone, all that I-know-where-I'm-going-and-am-going-to-get-there stuff you're usually so good at?' Then she groaned, something in the deep green eyes, the tightening of the pale features, making her bite her lip. 'I'm sorry, I was born with a big mouth and no brain!'

Hannah shook her head numbly. That was far from the truth; Manda had more insight than anyone else she knew. She should have spelled out the facts to Waldo, right from day one. But all along the line he had had her in a state of confusion that was totally alien to her, so alien that she hadn't known how to cope with it.

'I suppose you don't have his London number?' Manda rose fluidly to her feet, refilled their glasses and crossed to one of the long windows, pulling aside the deep blue velvet curtains, staring out at the dark wet night, shaking her head at Hannah's low negative response. 'Pity, you could have called him, told him you were planning to see Lottie this weekend. Told him what a disaster Eden was. Can't think why you didn't as soon as you knew why he'd hijacked you.'

'Pride, I suppose,' Hannah said dispiritedly. She had precious little of that left now. 'I didn't think I owed an explanation of my behaviour to anyone, least of all him. And then I fell in love with him and everything changed.

I couldn't bring myself to hurt him, and the truth about Eden would have done that—badly.'

Manda smiled wryly at the bitterness in Hannah's voice but added reassuringly, 'You could always get his phone number from Eden's father, David, isn't it? Then get in touch, tell him you've seen Lottie, and let him take it from there.'

Which was, Hannah admitted, a possible option. But did she really want to see Waldo again? Oh, she wanted to, all right, wanted it with every breath she drew. But would it be sensible? Because even if he did discover the truth about Eden, about herself, would he ever return her feelings? He had desired her, there was no doubt about that, but only because he believed she was morally loose, available to any man who turned her on.

That diagnosis didn't exactly flatter his character, but Hannah couldn't believe that a man of his drive, his dazzling sexual magnetism—a man who walked on the wild side—would be remotely interested in her as she truly was: quiet, serious, Hannah Sloane. Prim Hannah Sloane, pompous and priggish enough to believe that her precious feelings must be carefully protected from the chaos of love, the needs, the desires, the rapturous, unthinking act of giving.

No, Waldo Ross would never be even slightly interested in a woman like that. Unconsciously, she shook her head, missing the flicker of real concern in Manda's eyes.

Saturday was bright, a cloudless day, blue skies, the sunshine thin but welcome. Manda's red Mini covered the miles sweetly and Hannah's spirits lifted a little. At least she was doing something positive, and after she'd seen Lottie, the saga would be closed. No doubt David would let Waldo know she'd been—for what that was worth.

They would have come full circle and Waldo could put her out of his mind, forget all about her—if he hadn't already done so—and she could forget him. End of story.

But, for all that, she curled up inside at the thought of never seeing him again, never hearing that smoky, sexy voice. And she knew, with an insight that was acutely painful, that the plans for this journey had germinated a seed of hope. Hope that Waldo might be at the farm, that she would earn his approval for voluntarily doing what he'd wanted of her.

She was a weak-minded fool, a spineless idiot, she told herself bitterly. What had happened to that damned great wall she had vowed to erect between them? Build it high and build it thick, she'd promised. Yet what was she doing? Running to David and Lottie, hoping he would be there, or that, at the very least, they would give her news of him. She ought to be glad he hadn't bothered to contact her, toasting herself in champagne because it looked as though she would never have to see the devil again!

She almost turned back then, her disgust with herself making her grip the wheel as if she were about to wrench it off the steering column. But she was concerned about Lottie, particularly after what Waldo had said, and so she went on.

David was emerging from a large modern barn as Hannah pulled the Mini to a halt in the stackyard. He turned, a tall upright man in a dark blue boiler suit. A narrowing of deep grey eyes and then a tentative smile that went a little way to relaxing his lined, tired face.

'Hannah?'

He had aged, she thought compassionately as she slid out of the car, smoothing the skirt of the soft cashmere suit she wore, the colour of primroses.

'You look like spring.'

His eyes, his smile, were so like Eden's, she almost wished she hadn't come. It was going to be more painful for them all than she'd imagined. If they believed whatever Eden had told them about her, and they obviously did or they wouldn't have passed it on to Waldo, then they must hate her. And if she tried to exonerate herself, told them the truth, wouldn't they end up hating her even more for tarnishing his memory?

But, striding across the yard towards her, David didn't look as though he hated her. Uncomfortable, yes; that, but nothing stronger. She took the hand he held out, its strength surprising her, and she said gruffly, 'I hope you don't mind my turning up like this, but Waldo told me Lottie wanted to see me.'

'Mind?' His eyes clouded briefly then he turned, walking her towards the rear door of the big red brick farmhouse. 'It's good to see you again,' he tagged on, almost shyly. And then, 'Lottie's not been herself for a while now. She's had a lot on her mind, one way or another, though she never talks about it, but I know she'll be pleased you came.'

He pushed open the white painted door, standing aside to let her enter, and the sunny farmhouse kitchen enfolded her in a welcome she had almost forgotten.

'Mind you——' David was removing his muddy boots, reaching for slippers '—she did perk up when Waldo—Donald, we used to call him—came home.'

Predictably, the mention of his name made her heart pick up speed, and her mouth felt dry, her tongue clumsy as she asked, not quite daring to hope, 'Is he here now?'

'Not now.' He straightened up. 'I'll put the kettle on for a cuppa. I dare say you could do with something after the drive. No, he's back in Hong Kong, winding up some affairs there, so he said. We're not expecting him back for another two or three weeks. Not that he'll stay here for longer than a night or two. He'll probably open up the cottage he uses—it's not far away and he prefers to be independent. Always did, even as a lad.'

Hannah's throat tightened as memories of the cottage came winging back and David mistook her shuttered expression for weariness.

'Soon have the tea brewed.' He smiled at her, his eyes sad. 'And you'll stay to eat—overnight, if you like. I'll give Lottie a shout.' He was back moments later, looking pleased, younger. 'She's thrilled you've come! She's in the sitting-room and wants you to go through. Here, take your cup, and hers. Can you manage?'

She could manage blindfold, she thought, as she took the two cups and wove her way past the polished oak dresser in the large dim hall, past the side-table which always bore flowers—a pot of white cyclamens now, perfect and fragile. Holding the tray in one hand, she tapped on the sitting-room door, her pulses hammering uncomfortably. David didn't appear to bear a grudge, but Lottie might be a different matter.

Waldo had vowed to make her confront the havoc she had supposedly left behind. Lottie. The woman who had withdrawn into herself, the woman who hated her because she believed she had as good as killed her only, her beloved son.

Steeling herself to enter, Hannah plastered a smile on her face and pushed the door open. Lottie Wilmott was sitting in an upright chair near the window and the uncompromising spring sunlight showed just how much she'd changed since Hannah had seen her last.

'I've brought tea.' It was an inane thing to say, but it was all Hannah could think of. She put the tray down on the small table in front of the window beside an open sewing-box and met Lottie's eyes.

Once she had been a pretty woman, well dressed, carefully made-up, preserving her years. But no amount of make-up would hide the ravages of a rapid weight loss, the lines of anxiety deeply etched on to the faded face. And Lottie, as if reading her thoughts, whispered, 'I look a mess. But—but you are beautiful, as always.' And then, her voice stronger, 'I'm so glad you came. I wanted to ask you to come, but I couldn't bring myself to.'

'I know. Waldo told me.'

'He did? Oh, God!' Unstoppable tears poured down the grey cheeks, as if a tap had suddenly been turned on, and Hannah reached out a hand.

'Don't cry. Please don't cry.'

'It's stupid, I know, but it serves me right!'

Lottie's face contorted and she scrubbed her eyes with her sewing. 'Waldo—an outlandish name, we thought,' she laughed shakily. 'We used to call him Donald. If David and I had had another son he would have been named Donald. But there was only Eden. When did you see Waldo? I didn't know you'd met.'

Using delaying tactics, Hannah poured tea and passed a cup to the older woman. Once again the truth would have to be edited. And Lottie's attitude puzzled her. She had offered none of the vilification she had used on that other, fraught visit Hannah had made. And although she was undeniably upset, she certainly didn't seem to hate her now. So she told Lottie as much as she could, minimising Waldo's antagonism, editing out the passion, the hatred, her sudden blinding love for him.

'So he just whisked you away!' Lottie's eyes were dry now, wide, but not incredulous. 'He's always done what he believed he should, regardless of the opinions of others. He has a very determined mind of his own, that one. Wild. But his heart's big.'

And now was the time to put matters straight, tell Lottie the truth and hope, foolishly hope, that it might get back to Waldo, allow him to view her from a different perspective. The truth, coming from Lottie, would be easier for him to come to terms with. And then, knowing the truth, he might allow the undeniable male/female awareness that had been between them from the first to grow, broaden its parameters. There might be hope for her then. Hope for the now hopeless love that nothing seemed to diminish.

But for that to happen, she was going to have to tell this poor woman that her only son, her much loved son, had been—— She bit her lip, practically drawing her own blood.

The truth would have to come from Lottie; Waldo would never believe it if it came from Hannah herself. He had made it abundantly plain that he believed her to be nothing but a liar and a cheat. But how could she do it? How could she shatter beautiful memories, memories that could never be made whole again? Memories were all Lottie seemed to have now. Surely it was better to leave the truth unsaid; the truth was too harsh.

'It was all my fault,' Lottie whispered shakily. 'If I hadn't told him what I did, he wouldn't have done what he did. He has always carried a deep sense of obligation towards me. Unnecessary, of course, but there it is.'

Leaving her own tormented train of thought with difficulty, Hannah reassured her. 'You were understandably upset; you weren't to know that Waldo would take it on himself to deliver me here.' She was shaken to the core when Lottie groaned, 'I was wicked. Wicked!'

Lottie was shot to pieces emotionally and Hannah got to her feet. It had been a mistake to come. This meeting had done nothing but bring unhappy memories back. She said gently, 'I'm sorry. Try not to upset yourself so. I'll fetch David.'

'No!' The response was vehement, the plea in the older woman's eyes undeniable as she reached across the table to put a hand on Hannah's arm. 'David doesn't know what I said; I couldn't bear it if he found out. I've given the poor man enough to worry about as it is. Please listen.'

'Of course.' Hannah sank back on the chair, compassion for the other woman stirring deeply. 'What's wrong, Lottie?'

'Everything.'

There was remorse in the quiet voice and Hannah commanded softly, 'Tell me.'

'Yes.' Lottie nodded slowly. 'It's difficult, but I know I have to.' Shaky fingers were clenching and unclenching in the sewing on her lap. 'I've been hoping you'd come, for such a long time, but I couldn't bring myself to ask you. And like a fool, in a weak moment, I told Waldo that. If I've started one letter to you, then torn it up, I've started a hundred.' She took a deep breath, the words spilling out now. 'I said some terrible things when you came here after Eden died. I told lies—such wicked lies— and it's my fault Waldo did what he did. He must have been worried silly about me. Oh, Hannah, I've known about Eden for years! Can you ever forgive me? I knew he was weak. Sensitive, talented—but weak. I found out about the gambling and the debts while he was at university. The drink problem came later.

'I——' Her voice faltered and tears spilled unheeded as she met Hannah's incredulous eyes. 'We'd loved him so much, David and I, and I tried to help him. I kept it from his father—the worry would have killed him—and I didn't tell Waldo. He was away then, on the other side of the world, laying the foundations of the empire he was to build later.'

'I didn't know you knew,' Hannah said chokily as a strange kind of relief flooded her mind. There was no question, now, of the cruel choice between either having to disillusion Lottie or shouldering the blame for what had happened herself.

'I've known for years.' Lottie's voice was stronger, as if sharing the pain had made it easier to bear. Her hand went to her empty teacup and Hannah refilled it. Her eyes misted with pity for the burden Lottie had carried alone for so long.

'Perhaps Waldo could have helped,' she suggested, remembering the strength of the man, his fondness for Eden.

'No "perhaps" about it,' Lottie replied sadly, taking up her cup with two shaking hands. 'All I had to do was write and explain and Waldo would have come running. But that's easy to say, with hindsight. At the time, I didn't want him to know. The two boys had always been close: Eden idolised Waldo, and if Waldo had known of Eden's weakness then Eden would have felt so ashamed. You see, Waldo was always the strong one. Determined, always so determined. He never knew what weakness felt like. Even when he first came here, at nine years old, he had the strong-mindedness of a wild animal

fighting for survival. He was illegitimate,' she told
Hannah. 'His mother was a real madam—the child had
had one "uncle" after another. Heaven only knows how
he was treated, he's never spoken about it, but his mother
finally deserted him when he was seven. Left him in a
queue for fish and chips and never came back. The police
traced her as far as Leeds before the trail went cold, and
Waldo was put into care. He'd been in four different
foster homes before he came to us.'

'Dear God!' Green eyes glittered with unshed tears.
No wonder he now viewed a lack of morality in women
with undisguised disgust. He had believed Hannah
herself to be no better than the mother who had so cal-
lously abandoned him all those years ago. Only this time
it had been Eden, not he, who had been tossed aside,
wounded. 'But Lottie, why did you tell Waldo that I had
broken the engagement because I was some kind of
promiscuous tramp?' she asked, trying to keep her voice
level, free from ice.

'Because I'm a stupid, wicked old woman!' The
answer came fiercely, surprising Hannah by its violence.
'And I can't expect you to forgive me, but I hope you'll
try to understand. I was so happy when you and Eden
got engaged—David and I had both grown to like you
so much during that summer. And I thought Eden would
settle, change, if only a good, caring woman would take
him on. And I knew you were both. I'd done all I could,
but it needed a miracle. I saw you as that miracle. And
I was almost out of my mind with worry when he told
me you'd broken the engagement.'

She stared out of the window, her eyes lost. 'He also
told me he was in big trouble. The usual gambling debts.
He seemed more concerned about what those men he
spoke of would do to him if he couldn't raise the money,

than he was over the broken engagement. When I asked
him why you'd called it off he told me you were a two-
timing tramp, only interested in sucking a man dry. He
had no more to offer you and so you'd thrown him over
for someone else. I didn't believe that, and I guessed
you'd found out about the gambling, the drink. Then
Eden asked me for money, and I couldn't let him have
any more without his father knowing—and I didn't want
poor David worried and shamed. So I said I'd try to sell
the shares my mother had left me—that he must try to
keep those men quiet for a little while longer. But he
died. Drunk behind the wheel of a car. My son.'

'Oh, Lottie!' Impulsively, Hannah left her seat and
put an arm round the other woman's quivering
shoulders, laying her dark head against the grey one. 'If
only you'd told me when Eden and I got engaged. We
might have been able to work something out.'

'But you wouldn't have wanted to marry him if I had,'
Lottie pointed out. 'He did tell you, though, in the end?'

'Yes. He asked for a large sum of money, suggested
I sold my flat to raise it. I asked him why he needed it.
I couldn't understand, he seemed so different. It made
me sick. I tried to help him, but I couldn't——'

'No one could.' Lottie covered Hannah's hand with
hers. 'You mustn't feel guilty. No one could help Eden
because he couldn't begin to help himself. I saw that too
late. When he died, I felt I'd failed him. I blamed myself,
tried to blame you. But it was no one's fault but Eden's—
only I couldn't come to terms with that. All I could see
was the waste. Then Waldo came home, so strong, so
kind, and because I was half out of my mind with grief,
with knowing what I knew about my son, I repeated to
Waldo the reasons Eden had given me for the broken
engagement. David had been told the same lies but I

knew in my heart that the things Eden had said about you were untrue—although, at the time, I couldn't bring myself to admit it. Eden was dead, and the whole sorry tragedy had to be someone else's fault, not his. Can you understand that?'

'Yes, I think I can.' Hannah paced the room, pausing at last to stare out over the ploughed fields, the thin spring sunlight slanting through the bare branches of the oak trees that bordered the drive to the front of the house. 'You've lost one son, but you still have Waldo,' she said softly. 'Judging from the way he treated me he must love you very much. He believes I was indirectly responsible for the way Eden died and, by implication, responsible for your grief.'

'Yes.' Lottie got to her feet. 'I must do something about that. After Eden died I closed myself in with my grief, my own guilt, and I could talk to no one because no one knew the truth. I wanted to see you, to apologise, but I was too ashamed of what I had said to you to ask you to come. Waldo knew that I needed to see you, but he didn't know why. So he did what he did, and I must let him know how wrong I was. I must tell him the truth.'

She walked slowly to the door, making a visible effort to pull herself together. 'Now that I've seen you, explained, I can go on. And I still have David.'

# CHAPTER NINE

IT WAS late when Hannah got back to London, and because she knew Manda needed the car in the morning she parked it outside the mews cottages. And briefly, in the glare before she doused the headlights, she saw Manda, swathed in white fur, appear on her doorstep.

'Have a good trip?' Manda called as Hannah eased herself stiffly from the driving seat. 'Did darling little Lover's Gift go well? I'm only just home myself.'

Hannah tossed her the keys, smiling. Manda *would* refer to the new red Mini by the absurd name of Lover's Gift, even pretending not to remember the name of the man who'd given it to her. But Hannah knew Manda still saw more of James Pennington than she did of any other man, that she cared for him more than she would admit.

The model caught the keys. 'Thanks, sweetie,' and turned, wriggling deeper into her furs. 'Ye Gods, it's cold—I won't keep you now but I'll want to hear all about today—and what progress you've made with that beautiful man!'

The door closed behind her with a heavy clunk and, as if on cue, the 'beautiful man' moved out of the shadows near the adjoining doorway. There was nothing remotely beautiful about his expression. Savagely satanic was nearer the mark, Hannah thought incisively as her heart pounded heavily with the shock of seeing him when everyone believed he was still in Hong Kong. Her tongue clung to the roof of her mouth, making speech impossible—even if she could have thought of anything to say, which she couldn't.

'So you're sinking your claws into someone else.' His words bit out clearly in the still, cold air. 'Care to give me the progress report your friend couldn't make time for at the moment? I've got all the time in the world.'

There was little light, only starshine and a muted reflection from the street lamps in the road beyond the mews, but there was enough to show her the glittering savagery of black eyes, the indented lines at either side of the hard male mouth.

And those eyes burned with a strange fire as he bit out, 'Angling to get a bigger and better car from the latest dupe? Who donated that one? Gerald Orme? Eden?'

He looked as though he would like to tear Manda's bright little Mini to shreds with his bare hands, but contented himself with a look that would have melted the metal if sheer anger could be transformed to tangible force.

'Oh, dear God.' The words escaped her white lips on a shuddering breath that was dragged from her very soul. Lottie knew, had always known, of the darker side of Eden's character, and Lottie had promised to tell Waldo the truth when next she saw him. But what was the point? He hated her and it went so deep that it wouldn't be uprooted by a few words from her, from anyone. In his mind he had her grouped with his mother, an upmarket version, maybe, but still a tramp, a thing of no worth.

Physical and spiritual tiredness drained her, and his implacable anger, his hateful assumptions, added the *coup de grâce*. He approached her silently and she sagged against the cold metal of the car. She was reduced to a mass of instincts and they told her she needed to be alone, needed to find the oblivion of sleep. She said wearily, 'Go away.'

'The hell I will!' The response was immediate, determination jutting his jaw, and she shuddered.

'Why are you here?'

'Business.' Long hard fingers took her arms, pulling her upright. She tried to push him away and failed miserably. The instinctive side of her, the side that had led her to fall blindly in love with him, had been aching to see him again, but the rational part of her brain kept on insisting that he threatened her, told her to be rid of him, once and for all. But she was too tired to think straight and she stared at him blankly, paling at the sheer antagonism she saw stamped on his features.

'Business? At this hour?'

'At any hour, if I so choose it.'

At any other time the arrogance of that remark would have infuriated her. As it was, she felt too diminished to do more than make a protesting mumble at the back of her throat as he propelled her towards her door.

Finding her keys in a handbag that seemed full of the most irrelevant rubbish was an experience that added humiliation to the rest of her woes, and fitting the key in the lock an impossibility until he took it impatiently from her unresisting fingers and did the job for her.

Once inside, the sheer animal magnetism of the man, the presence, the power, filled the room she called home, making the well-known surroundings seem alien, out of focus, part of the dream world where only he was real. He drained her, yet she loved him. Fool!

Passing the back of one hand over her aching forehead, she asked him woodenly,

'What is it that couldn't wait until morning?'

He dragged her down still further with the acid comment, 'My God, you and the so-called beautiful man must have had a heck of a day. You're out on your feet!'

If only he knew! She could try to explain everything, but what was the point? She sank into a chair, her legs seemingly turned to jelly. The long hours spent driving, the emotional interview with Lottie, the need to appear cheerful during the meal they'd all eaten together afterwards, had proved to be exhausting. Even David's comment as he'd seen her to the Mini on her departure: 'I'm glad you came. Lottie's brighter than she's been since Eden went—and I want you to know that I, for one, never believed you were as black as the lad painted you. Your reasons for breaking the engagement would have been good ones,' had only sustained her spirits for a short while.

And now, when she needed to crawl into bed and seek the blessed oblivion of sleep, he was here, his presence alone building tension, creating havoc. She loved him and he loathed her, and for the life of her she couldn't dredge up the spirit, the energy, to explain that the Mini belonged to Manda, that she had the use of it on the rare occasions when she needed her own wheels, provided she left it with a full tank of petrol. That she had borrowed the car today to visit Lottie. As usual, he had come to all the wrong conclusions and, as far as he was concerned, she had to be public enemy number one.

Stiffening her spine, she looked up and found his eyes on her, his expression unreadable, and he told her, coming just a little closer, his feet making no sound on the soft grey carpet,

'I want Eden's unfinished manuscript.'

For a long moment she struggled to understand him, but her brain felt hopeless, like wet cotton wool. And then she shrugged, annoyance beginning to surface at last.

'Apply to the agency during normal working hours.'

'It's not here?'

'Why should it be?' She countered the disbelief in his tone with a show of asperity. 'After Eden's death Gerald and I didn't think it would be in any way helpful to return it to his parents. It's at the agency, and you may collect it at any time. And why do you want it?' Her brow wrinkled tiredly. It was almost too much effort to frown. 'You know it's unfinished, and even if it were it would be unpublishable.'

'You won't mind if I decline to take your judgement as final, your integrity as unimpeachable?'

He was apparently lost in contemplation of a water-colour above the hearth, soft blues and greens, a seascape chosen to complement her choice of décor, but he turned, catching the hurt expression she hadn't been able to control and she whispered, despair showing in the dejected lines of her body,

'You don't let up, do you? White's white and black's black and I'm the blackest of them all.'

She closed her eyes, not wanting him to see how misery was eroding her, eating away at her defences. The silence was total until, minutes later, she heard him clattering around in the kitchen. Why he should be in there, and what he was doing, she hadn't the energy to find out.

Today had been traumatic, from all viewpoints, and her love for him was counter-productive, draining her more than even his hatred did. She could very well understand how his early years had fostered this implacable dislike of the type of woman he believed her to be, this driving need to prove himself at the expense of everything else.

But just supposing—she sagged deeper into the chair—supposing she could summon up the energy to tell him that his suppositions regarding her character, the effect she had had on Eden, were wrong—what then?

He wouldn't believe her, so there was no point in trying to explain. But he would believe Lottie, and Lottie would tell him the truth. And after that she would see him no more because the only reason he'd made contact with her, past or present, had been because of his need to punish.

She felt his presence in the room even before the silence was broken by the chink of china as he put a tray down on a low rosewood table. And she opened her eyes, tentatively, sucking in her breath through her teeth because somewhere along the line he had discarded his sheepskin and the strength and grace of the lean hard body in black narrow-fitting trousers and a charcoal cashmere sweater had the power to bring every one of her senses alive as nothing else ever had or would.

'I made coffee,' he told her unnecessarily, pouring, handing her a cup. 'And I found brandy. You look as though you need it. Come——' He took the glass of dark amber liquid from the tray and held it to her lips, and she turned her head away in silent protest, sending the coffee cup flying, spilling the scalding contents over the primrose yellow suit. David had said she looked like spring, and now she felt like death.

Waldo swore softly, his eyes narrowing as he pulled her to her feet. 'You need a bloody keeper! Either that, or history is making sure it repeats itself.'

She bit her lip at that reminder, at the wryness in his voice. She felt utterly stupid.

'Get out of those things,' he commanded. 'Are you scalded?' This last with a trace of anxiety she knew had to be false. He wouldn't care if she roasted in hell. He had said so, once.

But she rallied, trying to retrieve some dignity from an encounter that had had all the cards stacked against her since Manda had unwittingly put new and damning ideas into his mind. And his mind was already receptive enough to any bad thing that was presented to it in regard to her.

'Yes, I'll have to change. Let yourself out, would you? And call in at the agency any time for Eden's manuscript.'

As an exit line it had its merits she thought, not much caring, doing her best to hold herself erect as she left the room. The expensive suit was ruined, and she didn't care about that, either. Waldo would have gone by now and she could crawl into bed and sleep. She might even sleep without dreaming of him—if the gods were with her, just for once.

She stripped in the bathroom, too tired to do more than brush her teeth, dragging the pins from her hair, releasing the chignon.

Dragging a fresh fine lawn nightdress from the airing cupboard, she pulled it over her head, turning away when she caught sight of herself in the mirror, the riotous black of her long thick hair emphasising her pallor, the hollows beneath her slanting cheekbones, the smudges of fatigue beneath her eyes.

Sweet heavens, she looked a mess! Dragging her weary body to her bedroom she flicked on the table lamp, knowing she'd have to read something light and amusing if she was ever going to put her mind into neutral, receptive to sleep.

She was standing, simply standing, as if her body was incapable of obeying her brain's instructions to get into

bed and pick up her book, when the snick of the opening
door had the hairs on the nape of her neck standing on
end, her body tensing even as she swung round.

'Get out of here!'

She might as well have commanded a stone to get up
and dance, might just as well, because he just kept
coming, the glass of brandy in one hand, his face unreadable as the dark eyes appraised the slender contours
of her body—contours she knew were shown to full advantage by the accident of the perfectly placed back
lighting, damn it!

'I've seen you wearing less,' was his comment, suave,
faintly amused. 'You look done in and I like my women
energetic, so why don't you just hop into bed and let
me look after you, just this once, as you once looked
after me?'

He was still coming and unless she wanted him to put
her to bed—which she knew he darned well would—she
had better do it herself. So she did, and he tucked her
up gently, punching the pillows. As he loomed over her,
the clean male scent of him stirred her senses, brought
back memories of exactly how she had looked after him,
cradling him in her arms all night, offering him the
softness of her body for his comfort.

'There now.' His voice was light, without inflexion,
as he arranged the supporting pillows behind her, his
fingers straying amid the tendrils of her hair. 'Relax
Hannah, just relax. The brandy will help you sleep. As
soon as you've finished it, I'll leave.'

Mistrusting him, she took the glass he held out. What
was with this new mood of kindly concern? He couldn't
stand the sight of her, and yet he was being kind. It
didn't make sense.

He made no attempt to touch her, except with his eyes, and they, she noted with rising panic, were touching every inch that was displayed above the sheets. Touching, lingering, searing; she drank shakily, preferring his anger or indifference to the seduction of his eyes. He was turning on the charm, for some reason best known to himself, but it was a surface thing. She could feel the underlying tension. Brandy-emboldened, she said bluntly, 'Why are you trying to be nice to me? It confuses me.'

'Because I want you. I know what you are and despite that, I want you. It confuses me, too, if it's any consolation.'

'Honest, at least.' There was a tightness in her throat. Tears. The tightness hurt, threatened to strangle her in her own misery. She wanted him, too, because she loved him. So she could understand that all-powerful need. But not like this. Not with the bitter commingling of desire and hate she felt coming from him.

'You make me sick.' She turned away, the pillow cool beneath her burning cheek, and put her fingers up to touch her face. Her skin felt hot, like fire, but there was a core of ice forming deep inside her and it hardened, consolidated as his voice came from the open doorway, grittily textured.

'I feel that way about myself. You sap my pride.'

# CHAPTER TEN

THE telephone rang out on Monday morning just as she was ready to leave the flat for the journey across the centre of London to the agency. It was Manda, only just surfacing from sleep by the sound of it, but sounding infinitely more cheerful than Hannah felt.

'I tried to get you all day yesterday,' Manda told her, a yawn in her voice. 'You must have been out.'

Hannah declined to reply to that. She had slept late yesterday, waking heavy-eyed, and had spent the day introspectively with her thoughts. They hadn't been easy company. She loved Waldo and was an emotional mess because of her involvement with this savagely intransigent man. She wanted him, and that chemistry was a two-way equation, but whatever she did or said he wrong-footed her.

There was no future for her as far as he was concerned and if she possessed half the strength of mind she had always prided herself on having she should be able to push him out of her heart, her mind, no hassle. That Lottie would one day tell him the truth had to be irrelevant. The way he instinctively viewed her, the blackly turbulent feelings she released from the private brooding core of his mind, conjured an image of the woman she would always be, to him. For Lottie to rearrange that image, kaleidoscope-fashion, would not alter a thing, not in the long term, because the components would always be there, unalterable, a fact of life as his mind had made them.

'Are you still there?' Manda's voice came suspiciously and Hannah shook her head in an effort to dispel the grey mists that clouded her mind, her reactions.

'Sure. What can I do for you?'

'Come to my party tonight,' came the prompt assertive reply. 'It's for James—it's his birthday.' There was a marked softening of tone at that and Hannah smiled, her suspicion that James Pennington—the generous donor of 'Lover's Gift'—wasn't as forgotten as Manda liked to pretend he was.

'Wouldn't he prefer a quiet dinner for two?' she put in slyly and Manda snorted, 'I'm a party person. He'll have to get used to that. I've invited all the neighbours, so they can't complain at the noise, and loads of super people. Eight o'clock and I won't take any excuses. See you.'

Hannah wrinkled her nose as she replaced the receiver. Having to present a bright face at one of Manda's glitzy parties was about the last thing she wanted, but if she were to take up her life at the point where Waldo had fractured it, slip back into the pattern he had so powerfully disrupted, then Manda's party might be as good a place to start as any.

And three hours later, towards the end of a hectic morning, Waldo himself provided just the right incentive.

'I'll pick up Eden's manuscript from your flat this evening. Eight-thirty.'

Her stomach somersaulting, Hannah had to tighten her grip of the receiver as it almost slid through her fingers at the sound of his voice. Internal upheaval was doing terrible things to her, but no matter how the masochist in her yearned to see him again, she was not about to meekly comply to his every draconian command. Perish the thought!

Her voice was coated with ice as she told him, 'Pick it up from the agency any time. Or better still, give me your address and I'll post it.'

'No.' His terse monosyllable took the wind out of her sails, drained her shaky composure, and she hissed,

'Why not?'

'Because I am collecting it from your place tonight.'

Oh, the devil was suave, give him his due. She said, relishing it, 'You'll be wasting your time. I'll be out,' and would have slammed the phone down but he was in there first.

'Where?'

His aggravating assumption that he was entitled to answers sent her blood pressure up several notches and, even though she was aware of Gerald's light brown eyes on her from the other side of the cluttered office, she growled, 'At a neighbour's party. Where I intend to have a wild time. Satisfied?' and dropped the handset back on to the cradle, hoping the rattle splintered his eardrum.

'What was that all about?' Gerald wanted to know, his mouth lifting in a smooth smile as he looked at her hot, cross face. 'Or isn't it any of my business?'

'The family want Eden Wilmott's unfinished manuscript.' She turned to her typewriter. 'I'll post it off as soon as I get an address.'

'But we have an address, surely.' Gerald was on his feet, looking at his watch, and Hannah shook her head.

'It's the brother, Waldo, who's asking. Sending it via his parents would only raise ghosts.' She began to type, the keys rattling frenziedly, inaccurately, and she knew she'd have to start again as soon as he left for lunch.

'Come and have a bar snack.' He stood over her, hovering, and when she shook her head and indicated the fresh fruit she'd brought along, he snapped pettishly,

'You're going to turn me down once too often, babe.' And then, as a parting shot, just before he slammed out of the door, 'You won't avoid me tonight. Manda's invited me as well.'

And that didn't do anything to increase her anticipation for the evening ahead, Hannah thought waspishly as she ripped the paper from the machine and started again.

She made sure she arrived early for the party, half afraid that Waldo would take it upon himself, in his usual high-handed fashion, to call by as soon as he'd judged her to be home from work. Her excuse for her early arrival—a desire to help with the last-minute arrangements—was airily brushed aside by a radiant Manda who was still wrapped in a bath towel. Everything was done.

'Help yourself to a drink, sweetie, while I wriggle into my glam. And if we're lucky there'll be time for you to tell me all about Saturday. And by the way,' she paused, tall and graceful in the doorway, her vivid hair gleaming against the dark wood, 'I invited Gerald along. You two still a pair? Or has the beautiful man put poor Gerry's nose out? I would have invited him, too,' she added wickedly, 'if I'd known how to contact him. But if you're off Gerald there are plenty of absolute poppets expected so you can console yourself with one of them!'

As Manda left, Hannah poured herself an orange juice from a lavishly stocked temporary bar in the window alcove. The long, graceful room had been cleared for dancing and a low trestle, covered with sea green silk and laden with goodies which ranged from plover's eggs and curls of smoked salmon to wickedly rich trifles, ran the length of the room.

Taking her glass, she paced the floor, her heels making hollow tapping sounds on the bare polished boards. The delicately ornate overhead chandelier dropped glittering fragments of light on to the elegant sofas and chairs which were arranged in groups on the edge of the room, touching the jewel bright shades of the plushy cushions reposing on cream and honeysuckle and pale jade upholstery. And suddenly the peace of her surroundings was broken by more early arrivals and Hannah was kept busy taking coats and wraps, dispensing drink and small talk until Manda, exquisite in a heavy white satin sheath, took over.

Gerald arrived with a flurry of other guests, making straight for her with a sulky look on his face that she didn't care for at all, and then James Pennington came and there was a chorus of good wishes, the popping of champagne corks, and Hannah, finding her glass re-filled for the second time, was thankful she'd stuck to innocuous fruit juice for starters.

With James's arrival and Manda's elegant appro-priation of him, the party had come alive. The chand-elier was dimmed and there was music for dancing, and laughing chattering groups of people helped themselves to food and drink. And Hannah, determined at all costs to keep out of Gerald's way, was acting totally out of character, dancing and flirting with someone whose name she couldn't remember. But he had careless blond hair, laughing blue eyes and a face that would have done any film screen proud.

Tonight she had dressed with elegance and style, making a statement. Manda had taught her how to use make-up, subtly but surely emphasising the emerald depths of her eyes, the delicate modelling of flawless bone structure, the translucent quality of her skin which made an unforgettable contrast to the riotous tumble of long, glossy dark hair. The dress she had chosen to wear was shimmering black, dipping daringly at the back, the front seductively skimming neat breasts, the slender arch of her pelvis, clinging to her thighs.

And the light, sophisticated flirtation she had embarked upon was a statement, too, a firm denial of the stupid something deep inside her that was yearning for that lean dark devil who had shaken her safe little world until it had seemed in danger of total disintegration.

The large white zircon of her ring, the only ornament she wore, flashed coldly against the dark fabric covering her partner's shoulder, catching a refraction of light from the chandelier. It was like a warning, bringing her head up, her nostrils pinching as she instinctively scented danger.

The lean dark devil was here, damn him! Talking to Manda who was shaking her head, a laughing denial of something he had said as she leant back into the curve of James's arms.

But although he was talking to Manda his eyes were on Hannah as she swayed to the sensuous beat of the music. His mouth was smiling for Manda, but his eyes were sending quite different vibrations across the room. The sound of the music faded for Hannah, losing all meaning, and her body grew rigid with screaming tension, the central heating almost too warm, the scent of jasmine overpowering.

The blond man drew her closer, his head coming down as he said huskily, 'Let's give ourselves a drink, find somewhere quiet and sit the next one out.' But blind to all else, Hannah saw Waldo shoulder his way through the other slowly moving couples, felt his hand, hard and cool, on the burning skin of her arm.

'Excuse me.'

There was ice in the tone, and steel, and after bristling, pulling himself upright, the blond backed down, mumbling something incomprehensible, and walked away from the dark face that held murder.

The contact of his hard body, his arms as he pulled her close to him, moving explicitly to the beat of the seducing music, shocked her, making her flesh crawl with heat. Futilely, she tried to pull away, but his hand moved over the bare skin of her back, turning her to fire. There was nothing her weak body could do about the wicked closeness of him, a closeness that brushed her thighs, her belly, her breasts, making her mindless.

But she had a brain, a tongue in her head, and using her fading resources of willpower she lashed out thinly,

'Reduced to gate-crashing now? Can't any of your own friends stand you any more? Do you have to foist yourself on people who are too polite to throw you out?'

'Shut up, Hannah.' Both hands moved to the slender grace of her waist, drawing her hips so close to the hot pressure of his that she felt they'd been welded together. There were wicked, demanding glints in his eyes now, overlying the basic anger, and she closed her own, drifting defeatedly where he led her, her senses seduced by his touch, her mind neutralised.

She wasn't aware that he'd manoeuvred her through the door until the cooler air of the dimly lit vestibule slid over her heated skin. He was holding her in a lover's embrace, not dancing now to the faintly heard music, and although the sensations he'd aroused in her were an intolerable need, she tugged away from his encircling arms.

He told her grimly, 'Get your coat—whatever.'

Hannah stared at him, her stomach churning, her eyes still hazed with the physical effect he had on her, and he repeated, his lips tight, 'Get your coat. I'm taking you to dinner.'

'No.' The denial struggled out over the croak in her throat. 'I'm going back to that party.'

'Can't wait to get to grips with the golden boy again?' His eyes narrowed in a look that was more telling than any sneer and her stomach muscles contracted painfully. He was doing it again, wrong-footing her. It had been the story of their stormy relationship. She recalled all the caring he was capable of—for Lottie and David, for Eden, for the half-frozen robin. And she, who loved him, received only his contempt. Desire counted as nothing, in such circumstances.

'I want to talk to you, and I can't do it here. If we went to your place I'd end up making love to you, and much as I ache for that I need to talk to you first.' He bunched his hands into his trouser pockets, his black eyes dominating her. 'So we'll find neutral ground. Talk. Fetch your coat.'

Talk. Make love. She had no say in the matter, apparently. And he was right in his assumptions; she, weak fool that she was where he was concerned, would always end up doing exactly what he demanded!

She had slipped her sable jacket over her shoulders when she'd left her flat and she took it from the hall-stand, draping it over her shoulders in mindless compliance to his will. She didn't know what he wanted to talk about, she thought he had said it all, spilling out his venom at every encounter. But perhaps, if she listened for one last time, he would leave her in peace to get on with her life, to forget him, to lock away her love for him somewhere deep and hidden inside her heart, never allowing it to surface again.

Nothing was said as she walked at his side to his parked car, the icy remoteness of the stars overhead seeming to parallel their relationship: distant, cold, unattainable. And the silence in the cocooning warmth of his car as he drove her across London was no better: edgy, fraught with spiralling tension. Fleeting impressions imprinted images on her racing mind—street lights, traffic, his hands on the wheel, a dark-clad thigh close to her own, the spicy masculine scent of him, a quiet tree-lined square, discreet black and white awning, a liveried doorman moving down wide stone steps, opening the door at her side, his greeting for Waldo deferential.

A small flurry, not too obvious—suited to the quiet, opulent ambience—something said by a morning-coated manager, made her lift one eyebrow.

'You own this place?'

His silent avowal, shaking her somewhat. Soft lighting, warmth, thick luxurious carpets underfoot, an atmosphere of discreet luxury, understated wealth. A quiet table for two, candlelit, in an alcove, the number of other diners—the men formally dressed, contrasting dramatically with the glitter of jewels, the elegant turn of a smooth feminine shoulder.

Waldo ordered their drinks, their food, without consulting her or the huge leather-bound menu. Feeling superfluous, his cool disregard even more hurtful than his anger, she tried to pull herself together, to emerge from the strange trance-like state she had inhabited since he had taken her from the party.

She had to assert her personality. But it was difficult. He had manipulated her since that dark February morning when he had appeared at her door—'Miss

Sloane for Gatwick?'—and he had been manipulating her ever since.

She sipped her drink, a very dry Martini, and the stone in her ring caught the light, glinting coldly. As if that had caught his attention, he said wickedly, so smooth, so suave, so sure of himself,

'I have a proposal to make, but first a question.'

'Fire away.' Her mouth felt dry; she was shaken by the verbal contact after all that silence and she fixed her attention on the flickering candle in its crystal holder, not wanting to meet his eyes.

'Are you emotionally capable of remaining faithful?' He was leaning back, relaxed and cat-like, and she knew that, like a cat, he was waiting to pounce, to come in for the kill. His face was thrown into shadow, unreadable.

She said thinly, 'What kind of question is that?'

'One that needs an answer.'

Colour burned a defiant way along her cheekbones but she bit out, 'Of course I damned well am!' and her lashes flickered as her deep emerald eyes sought his with mute appeal. The lean perfection of his body was magnificently suited to the austerity of the black dinner jacket and black tie, the severe planes and angles of his face which the candleglow did nothing to soften. Her reply to his question seemed to harden the long line of his mouth.

'I could just about take what I know of your past. I don't have any choice,' he told her with a trace of wryness, a giving way that was alien to her knowledge of him. 'But I couldn't take it if it were translated to our future.'

The enigmatic words brought a thousand questions bubbling to the surface of her mind, too many to sort into order of precedence, remaining unspoken, anyway, as their first course was brought to the table. What future, for pity's sake? There wasn't one, not one that contained the two of them as an entity.

But she muttered, when they were alone again, 'I don't know what you're talking about,' then listened with an increasing sense of disorientation as he enlightened her.

'There's something between us that's too damned strong to ignore, Hannah. You know it, I know it. You're a fever that won't let me go. And God knows I've tried to talk some sense into myself.' He squeezed lemon over his smoked trout pâté, his fingers long, hard, remorseless. She shuddered, knowing the truth of what he'd said, and he told her,

'When Lottie told me how you'd hurt Eden, I was determined to find you, to make you pay. I saw you on several occasions before you met me that morning. And each time I got more involved. The biter bit, if you like. I found myself needing to dig into your past, get to know you, and eventually what started out as an intended tongue-lashing developed into abduction. I didn't acknowledge it at the time, even to myself, but you'd already got under my skin. And wanting the woman who'd emotionally crippled my brother wasn't something I was proud of, believe me. But I've come to terms with that, I've had to. So, as I see it, we have two choices—we burn, or we do something about it.'

'Like what?' Her mouth was parched, her throat constricted, and although common sense told her to get the hell out of here, find a taxi, leave while there was still time to make that choice, she couldn't move. Only her hands, twisting in the folds of the linen napkin on her lap, seemed capable of movement.

'Like exploring the possibility of a new depth to our fraught relationship.' His mouth moved in the first smile he had given her, paralleling the slight wry way his shoulder lifted. 'I want you with me and I won't pretend it would be easy. But nothing worth having is ever easy and you'd be a challenge to my image of myself——' Again the wry tug of his mouth, the close, watchful glance across the table. 'Am I man enough to hold the lovely wanton? That's about the humiliating gist of it. And my God, Hannah,' his voice was thick with sudden need, a thread of pain, 'I want to hold you in every sense of the word.'

It was too much, too audacious, and far too tempting. Her heart thudded wildly beneath the shimmering black fabric of her dress, an echoing pulse beating frantically at the base of her long ivory neck. And as her mushed-up first course was removed, another plate put in front of her, wine poured, rich and dark, she knew they had reached a watershed in this tormented relationship. A relationship that had bound them together since its unlikely beginning, yet torn them apart.

Some last shred of the self-respect that had kept her her own woman, answerable to no one except the dictates of her own conscience, her sense of self-worth, helped her to make one last stand.

'Are you suggesting that I wait around ready to make my body available whenever your urge to hold me overcomes your delicate scruples?' Ice in her voice, but fire in her veins, her control just sufficient to hide the havoc from him.

'No, no way. That isn't the kind of relationship I have in mind. That way, I'd never know for sure where you were, who you were with.' He topped up her wine glass, the fine hairs on the back of his hand very dark against the whiteness of a silk cuff. 'I want you with me, and it would be as permanent as your ability to remain faithful would let it be. I'd give you the option of keeping your career if you wanted it. As you know, I'm delegating more, basing my operations in the UK, so if you decided to continue at the agency we'd use my flat—it's larger than yours, more central for your work. And I'm looking for a place in the home counties—Eyesore's too remote for weekends.' He gave her a level look. 'If you decide to give up your job we might make it a permanent home. And in that event you'd need security, so the house I buy will be in your name. I can't be fairer than that. There's a cottage in Bucks I'm looking over on Saturday; you'd need to approve my choice. I'll give you the rest of the week to think it over. We burn, or you come to me, it's your decision. I'll call for you on Saturday at nine. If you agree to my proposal we'll take the day out, look over the cottage, take things from there. And if you make the trip with me, Hannah, I'll take it as a commitment on your part. If you don't, you'll never see me again.'

As a proposal of marriage, it had to be the coolest, most phlegmatic, she'd ever heard of. To be married to him until she was wrong-footed again, innocently arousing his jealousy and rekindling his feelings about the past he had dreamed up for her, thus driving him to divorce her, would be like living on a time bomb.

But loving him as she did, she wanted to spend the rest of her life with him, grow old with him, share his name, his highs and lows, his hopes and fears; have his love, his trust. This way, his way, having him physically but never spiritually, having his eyes on her, continually looking for signs of the wantonness he believed to be an intrinsic part of her character, with the love entirely on her side, would be killing.

But oh, she did love him! And wasn't the type of marriage he was so calmly, almost casually, offering better than nothing at all? And maybe in time, when he grew more sure of her, of her love, it would become a real marriage for him, too.

Vainly, she tried to pour cold logic on the fire that was her love for him. And, reluctantly, she lifted her eyes to his and saw that there was something different in the gold-flecked depths. Sexual awareness, yes, that— but something different, deeper, more profound. It was something beyond time, beyond place. It was for ever. And Hannah, defeated, acknowledged silently that she was well and truly lost.

# CHAPTER ELEVEN

So FAR the day had been a whisper away from perfection, Hannah acknowledged to herself as she looked out of the mullioned window in the empty master bedroom. Waldo's cottage had turned out to be an enchanting stone-built Tudor manor house, not too large, set in two acres of redeemable gardens. And he'd said, 'If you like it, it's yours.'

It had been the first time he had referred, even obliquely, to the proposal he'd made to her on the night of Manda's party, and the only acknowledgement he'd made of her commitment had been in the revealing glitter of black eyes as she'd been ready and waiting when he'd arrived at nine that morning. His easy conversation, his unforced charm, had relaxed her, smoothing what could have been a difficult moment. She had seen a new, lighter side of his character, and she liked it. She knew she had made the right decision when she'd surrendered her future to this man. At least, she thought she had. She would love him always, and where he went she would follow, and if she had allowed his charismatic personality, his male potency, to blind her to her inborn sense of caution, then so be it. It was fate, and who was she to fight it?

The sound of his footfall on the bare oak boards alerted her to his presence and she turned, her heart in her eyes.

'It's perfect, Waldo. Perfect.'

He had been inspecting the plumbing and there was a smear of dust on his high forehead, more on his hands and the knees of his denims. His voice was dry as dust, too, as he commented, 'Then it's settled. I'll get the wheels turning.' Something flickered in his eyes, tightened his mouth, and it frightened her.

Did he believe she had consented to be his wife because he'd offered to buy her a *house*! Who knew what went on behind those clever black eyes?

She shivered, the coolness edging between them for the first time that day, and as if he sensed its icy breath, too, he glanced at his watch, shrugging aside the creeping silence. 'Give me five minutes to get cleaned up and we'll find somewhere to eat.'

The village pub offered indifferent sandwiches—cheese only, the ham was off—but to Hannah they could have been food for the gods and when Waldo, pushing aside his barely touched plate, told her, 'I'll get a surveyor in and a good firm of restorers to follow his brief,' she closed her eyes, a small soft smile curving her mouth as she vividly recalled high raftered halls, smooth dark panelling, winding passageways and dim galleries. 'I don't want it changed, it's beautiful.'

'Not changed. Restored.' He leant back against the shabbily upholstered seat, lean, relaxed, utterly male, and Hannah's mouth went dry. She loved him so much, wanted him until the need was a pain, and not once today had he made any attempt to touch her. He was holding back, even though she had tacitly committed herself to him. But she, too, had been conscious of a wariness in herself that had kept the light impersonal interplay of looks and words right there on the surface. Yet underneath it all there was an undeniable sensation of something building, growing towards the inevitable climax that, when it came, would be cataclysmic.

Forcing a smile that trembled beneath the arcane scrutiny of veiled black eyes, she gulped at her cider, dry and sharp and tasting of sparkling summer days, and surfaced, almost babbling, 'It's large, for a weekend place. It should be a home—the hearth should never be cold.'

'Poetic?' He tipped a black arched brow. 'Or are you trying to tell me you'd consider making a home out here? What about your job? I don't need to tell you that I could keep you, that I'm in the fortunate position of being able to choose my own home base—within reason. I'll be keeping the London flat solely for your convenience if you want to continue with your career.' His long fingers played with a beer mat, his eyes holding hers with an intensity that filled her mind with thoughts that could not be transmitted to him, because as far as he was concerned she was still a tramp whose faithfulness could only be bought with material assets.

Of course she wanted to make her home at Moorgate Hall, with him, to turn the empty, lovely house into a real home, to fill the rooms with joy, with flowers, with love, make an enchanted haven for just the two of them, make a dream come true.

But dreams were for children and fools, and she was neither; one day he would tire of her, or believe her to be unfaithful, and on that day she would need her career because she would have nothing else. Although her job had toppled dramatically from the top of her list of priorities, she knew she would be crazy to let it go, relinquish it for a dream that had no substance.

Schooling her features to unconcern, she shrugged slightly. 'I'd have to think about that. I love my job. And talking of jobs,' she changed the subject, feeling for safer ground, 'Why aren't you in Hong Kong? I thought you weren't expected back for two or three weeks.'

'I changed my mind.' He accepted the change of subject but she was aware of how tightly he was stretched. 'I told you, I'm delegating more. I wanted to get this thing settled—for us. Anyway,' his eyes questioned sharply, 'how did you know about the proposed Hong Kong trip? Been checking me out?'

That was rich, coming from him! He had done enough checking on her and wouldn't, or couldn't, believe he'd come up with the wrong answers.

Masking inner sadness with a small smile, she shook her head. 'Lottie told me. She thinks you're still out there—unless you've been in touch recently?'

'No, I haven't,' he told her slowly, leaning forward, puzzled, oddly wary. 'When did you see her?'

'Last weekend. I borrowed Manda's car and drove over to visit. We got a few things sorted out. And when I got back you were waiting, and you thought some guy had given me the Mini for services rendered,' she tagged on for good measure, giving him something to think about. And if he'd bothered to get in touch with Lottie he would have learned that Eden hadn't been all white, she all black, but she didn't say that. The time to tell him about Eden was not now, not here. 'I think we ought to go before we get asked to leave. It's well gone closing time.'

She gathered her bag, stood up, rebuttoning the loose jacket of the finely woven trouser suit she wore, the simple style emphasising her slender grace, the rich peacock blue of the fabric deepening the green of her eyes.

His silence as he opened the creaky door of the bar for her, then followed her out to the pale spring sunlight, was thick with unvoiced questions and it lasted, redolent with the quiet thoughts that were being examined inside that well-shaped skull, for several miles.

Then he seemed to relax, as if he'd decided not to spoil a nearly perfect day, the first day of a future together that might be short enough without raking over past dirt—as he would see her mythical mercenary relationships with a string of lovers. 'Where would you like to eat this evening? My flat or a restaurant?'

Consideration for her preferences hadn't exactly been a strong point of his during the time she had known him, and she had the impression that he was doing his best to behave as though they were any ordinary couple who'd recently met, discovered a point of mutual physical desire and had decided to do something about it in a civilised manner.

And it was a farce. Whatever future they had together couldn't be founded on misunderstandings, a pretence that neither of them had a past or had complex reasons for being what they were at this moment in time. Everything, past, present and future, had to be taken into account, lived with. And to begin to sift the truths from the untruths she needed the courage that being on her own ground might give her.

'My place,' she said.

Hannah heard his footsteps on the stairs outside her flat and breathed in, exhaling slowly, trying to still the nervous patter of her heartbeats. Ever since he'd dropped her off, a couple of hours ago, she had been wound up, like a spring about to break.

She had showered, washed her hair, and now it fell softly over her shoulders, its untamed dark beauty spilling over the silver grey silk of the body-skimming caftan she had chosen to wear with heavy wrought silver chains at her wrists and throat. And because she'd left the door on the latch he walked right in, black eyes appraising, openly wanting.

'You look like a midnight witch. Black and silver, with green eyes to drown in.' He kissed her then, lightly, playing with her, his eyes softly mocking, the dark grey lounge suit, the ice-green crisp shirt and plain grey tie adding to his urbanity, presenting yet another facet of a character already complicated enough.

He had brought wine, flowers—two dozen long-stemmed scarlet roses. She took the blooms, her fingers trembling over the silky cool petals, knowing he was acting out a part he'd created for himself, for her. The sophisticated lover paying due homage to his lady. And it was wrong, so wrong!

'I'll put them in water. Help yourself to a drink.' Her voice was tight despite her best efforts to keep tension out, and she spent longer in the kitchen than was necessary, arranging the roses that seemed to mock her with a perfection her relationship with Waldo could never attain.

He was examining the spines of the books on her shelves, a glass of whisky in his hand, and she crossed silently to the drinks tray, needing something, sloshing a small amount of the whisky into a glass. He'd heard her, of course, and he turned smoothly on his heel, his expression quite, quite bland; she didn't know him.

'Don't you want to hear how Lottie was?' The unguarded words tumbled out, and he met them, the heat that crept up to her hairline, with a small sardonic smile.

'Not now. I want to eat, make plans for us, make love to you. But not necessarily in that order. Come here.'

She went, of course she went, mindlessly drawn to him as she knew she would always be. Went on shaky legs with a shakier will, melting into his arms as he reached out to her. His fingers drifted over her unsteady lips, his eyes intent as if memorising the contours through sight and touch, and he murmured smokily, 'Such a kissable mouth.' The fingers slid down her throat and her skin sprang to vital life where he touched it, moving down to the deep V of her neckline, straying beneath the silk, feathering over her skin before closing over one of her aroused breasts, sending deep shudders of aching response through her.

Gently, then with deepening passion, he took her mouth; her arms reached instinctively around him and she was returning his kiss hungrily, moulding her warm, pliant woman's body to the male thrust of his.

She was on fire for him and knew what he'd meant when he'd spoken of burning. But they were going to put that right, he'd said so, and he meant it.

'I want to kiss your body, taste every inch of it,' he groaned against the flushed skin of her cheek. 'I want to undress you, touch you, let my mouth and hands learn your body until my mind absorbs it, inch by delicious inch. I want to drown in your body, Hannah. Take you. Make you mine.'

His words, the expert play of his hands on the willing contours of her body as they blazed a trail of fire through the thin silk of her caftan, conjured mind images of blinding eroticism, and she groaned helplessly, her hands moving impatiently inside his jacket, finding the warmth of his hard male flesh beneath his shirt. He moved slightly away, taking both her hands in both of his, holding her apart from him. 'But not now. Later, my lovely wanton, later.'

It took a few moments for his words to sink in and when they did she turned stiffly away, hating him for his power to torment her, to reduce her to a helpless mass of desires, her mind, her intelligence, blotted out, swamped with need.

'I'll fetch the food through; it is ready,' she told him, trying to sound as though frustration weren't eating her alive. 'You'll find a corkscrew on the drinks tray.'

He was right, of course, they needed to talk, although he would doubtless disapprove of the subject matter she had in mind! Organising the meal hardly calmed her at all. She had hoped it might, but his seductive expertise had blown most of her control and her hands were still shaking as she carried in the dish of salmon steaks poached in white wine, the herb butter, crisp rolls, fresh salad.

They sat opposite each other at the table she'd set with such care before he arrived and, as candlelight glinted on cut crystal, polished silverware, jade china, she felt sucked into a world that contained only the two of them, the unspoken knowledge that before this night was out they would be lovers, his body knowing every inch of hers, hers knowing his.

He ate appreciatively, but Hannah was too aware of him, of the sexual tension that mounted second by agonising second, to do more than toy with the food and wine. Something intolerable was building up inside her and, sipping wine to ease the dryness of her throat, she almost choked when he laid aside his napkin.

'Thank you, Hannah, that was superb.' And then, in the same smooth tone, 'You excite me beyond endurance. Let me love you.'

'I——' She gulped, setting the glass down with unsteady hands, the answering need he provoked in her starting low in her stomach, spilling out to fill every part of her. 'We—we have to talk.' Drowned green eyes were raised to his with difficulty, then slid away as he said,

'Ah,' sagely. 'We need to lay the ground rules first. So be it.'

'I'll fetch the coffee,' she babbled, on edge, the smile she put in his general direction much too bright as she scrambled out of the room.

In the kitchen, where the coffee was perking and filling the space with its fragrant aroma, Hannah leant her hot forehead against the cool wall tiles. This got worse and worse! He was now thinking that she wanted everything laid on the line, her future payment for services rendered—quite apart from the gift of a Tudor manor house—all neatly spelled out! She doubted if he'd even blink an eyelid if she were to present him with a typed marriage settlement, ready for his signature. He didn't know that the only thing she wanted from him was his love—and no one, least of all Waldo, could lay any ground rules for that!

Without consciously thinking about it, she put the coffee things together on a tray, her mind fully occupied with the task of bringing some mental stiffening to a body that was apt to turn to jelly with one word, one look from him. And she had herself reasonably under control by the time she carried the coffee through; she was going to have that serious talk with him before things went any further.

Waldo was lolling back on the sofa, his indolent, cat-like grace stirring gooseflesh over her body. She put the tray on a low table in front of him and he patted the space at his side, his eyes gleaming with inner devilry.

She glanced quickly away before those glinting eyes could compound the shaming weakness that invaded her soul through every pore of her skin and she compromised, curling up at the opposite end of the sofa, her long legs tucked under her, holding her coffee cup like a shield.

Waldo acknowledged her tactical manoeuvre with the slight tilt of a dark brow and imparted, 'I'll take you to my flat tomorrow. It's strictly a bachelor pad—a touch sparse—so there'll be ample room for all, or any, of your own furnishings.' He stirred his coffee idly, his eyes drifting over her face, her body, searing, and she gritted her teeth to prevent the choking cry of need from leaping out of her constricted throat.

'I've already told you that you needn't keep your job on, unless you want to. And if you do decide to give it up we'll make Moorgate our permanent home as soon as the restorers move out.' He had finished his coffee and put the cup down on the tray, leaning forward, his hands dangling between his knees, his enigmatic eyes holding hers in a slanting sideways look.

Hannah tried to look away. She couldn't. And her heart thundered its own sweet, heavy beat because what he was offering, on the face of it, was magic. But there were depths beneath the shining surface that needed to be plumbed. And she had hardly begun to formulate the words needed to tell him so as he continued matter-of-factly.

'In any case, I want you with me. I'll organise a firm of removers this coming week. It shouldn't take you more than a couple of days to pack your personal things and decide what, if any, of the furniture you want to bring. You'll have a better idea of that after you've seen my flat tomorrow. I wouldn't want you to have to part with anything of sentimental value.'

He didn't believe in hanging around, she thought, the breath sucked out of her body by the pace he was setting, his single-minded intention to have her honour her commitment to move in with him. And he turned the screw another degree, adding silkily, 'Move in with me on Wednesday. Take the week off. That should give you time to get organised, contact the service people, your landlord.'

'I don't have a landlord,' she told him quickly. 'I would have to put the flat up for sale, or let it.' Caution edged her voice. She wouldn't feel safe doing either. She wasn't gullible enough to believe that her marriage to Waldo would last for ever, and she knew she was storing heartbreak for herself by taking what she could of him, feeding her love for him, while she could.

He looked at her blankly for a fragment of time before his eyes slitted dangerously. He leaned back into the angle of the sofa, one ankle resting on the knee of the other firmly planted leg. 'A bit rich, on your salary,' he commented witheringly, his hard lips barely moving, and Hannah felt the heat of anger stain her skin, could do nothing about it. He didn't know how much she earned but he could make a well-informed guess and no, there was no way she could have afforded to buy her own flat on her salary alone, good though it was.

She replaced her coffee cup on the tray, ashamed of the way her hands were shaking, clasping them together in her lap. Stiffly, she told him, 'I know what you're thinking—that it was bought by one of my many lovers.' But even the ice in her voice was not proof against him.

He cut in savagely, 'Leave it. I don't want to know. As from this morning we started out with a clean slate.'

It was on the tip of her tongue to tell him to get lost, to take his clean slate and do something painful with it. But this was too important for the luxury of an outburst of anger, much as it might have relieved her feelings.

'We can't build any sort of worthwhile relationship on lies, mistrust, misunderstandings,' she said calmly, hoping he would listen to the voice of sweet reason. 'To begin with, I don't have a string of lovers, past or present, and I bought the flat as an investment with my father's legacy.' She had hoped, by keeping her tone light, she would have begun to get him on her side, in a mood to listen to what had to come next. But his features might have been carved from granite, only a slight muscular movement along his hard jawline indicating that emotion of some kind dwelt in that finely shaped head.

'I don't doubt you have your reasons for thinking the worst of me. You listened to gossip, hearsay, overheard a conversation, and jumped to all the wrong conclusions. I don't entirely blame you, but you have to believe that I'm not like your mother, and if we're to have anything good together you've got to believe that you were wrong about me, totally, utterly wrong.'

'What the hell do you know about my mother?' His face had whitened, whether from shock or anger she had no way of telling. 'Lottie, I take it?'

She nodded mutely, compassion in her eyes. Digging into the past would be painful for him. 'Waldo, please listen to what I'm trying to say——'

Her words ended on a near squeak of desperation and she dragged in a shaky breath. His expression was completely stone now, conceding nothing, and the quality of still watchfulness that cloaked him was unnerving, to say the least. But she had to make him believe. 'I know you think I treated Eden badly. And maybe I should have tried harder. But he resented everything I said and did, didn't want my help.' Her hands twisted together and she could feel the damp skin clinging, palm to palm. Now was the moment of truth. Lottie had made sure that Waldo never knew of Eden's degeneracy, and now she was going to have to tell him, and it wouldn't be pleasant for either of them. 'If he had been crippled in a road accident, or by a disease, it would never have occurred to me to call the wedding off.'

She was fighting for them both, for a sign from him that he could understand. But he regarded her bleakly, the ungiving lines of his face defeating her. 'But Eden was crippled in a different way,' she began again, finding the courage from somewhere.

'Financially, you mean?' The words were spoken softly, but the distaste was undeniably there, stronger and more menacing for the quiet delivery. Hannah passed the tip of her tongue over parchment dry lips.

'No, psychologically. His mind was crippled, there was a sickness in him I couldn't live with. He was a compulsive gambler, almost an alcoholic. And if our marriage is to stand any chance at all, you have to believe me.'

'Marriage?' For a moment he looked stunned, his face dominated by ravaged black eyes, then he swung to his feet, his mouth twisted with anger. 'You sicken me!' He stood over her like an avenging angel, the violence in him implicit in tightly clenched fists, glittering black eyes, the savage line of his mouth. 'You anger me beyond sanity! Have you the least idea, you bitch, of what it cost me to overcome my scruples and freely admit I wanted you in my life? You can't have——' His upper lip curled derisively and Hannah sank back against the sofa, his hatred of her making her feel ill with shock. 'You haven't a scruple in your sickening armoury. I want you, you burn me up, and I was prepared, and you damned well knew it, to put the past behind us. Start clean. But no!' The fist of one hand cracked into the palm of the other, the sound of the impact reverberating inside her skull. 'You saw the financial advantages of keeping me sweet—the Hall, for starters, a life of luxury, ease if you wanted it—all yours for the taking. You only had to agree to put your past away, out of sight, stay true. But no, you bitch, you had to try and go one better. And you miscalculated there, because I'm not the type of guy even you can wheedle round. Especially not when you try to do it by blackening my brother's character!'

He touched her then, taking her ashen face in one iron hand, black eyes probing the wide orbs of tear-glistening green, and he whispered savagely, 'Goodbye, lady. You just lost yourself a well-intentioned, well-heeled lover.'

She struck out at him, at the bitter crudity of his words, but he caught her flailing arm, holding it in a grip she thought might break the bone. She bit her lower

lip with pain, sucking in her breath, and he moved his
hand, flinging her arm away so that it fell, like a rag-
stuffed object that had nothing to do with her, impotently across her shuddering body.

'Better luck next time, lady. And if you'll learn not
to hit below the belt you might pull it off another time.
But not with me.'

He turned on his heel and stalked out, banging the
door behind him, out of her life for ever, but not out
of her heart, damn him!

# CHAPTER TWELVE

HANNAH stripped off her sodden blouse and skirt and dropped them in the linen basket; the ice-blue satin bra and briefs followed them and, shivering, she stepped under the stingingly hot shower. The day had started bright and warm, but as she'd left the tube station on her way home from work the skies had been full of sullen fury and the cloudburst had caught her unprepared.

She hadn't felt like going with Manda to the party James was holding at his place, staying overnight because it would probably go on until dawn. Now, after getting thoroughly chilled and soaked, she knew she was going to have to cry off. She felt like death.

Out of the shower, she rubbed herself dry then pulled on a thick terry bathrobe, wrapping the long, wet strands of her hair in a towel. She paused as her huge shadowed eyes met their mirrored reflection. She looked like death.

The shower hadn't relaxed her; nothing did, not since Waldo had stormed out of her life three weeks ago. She had lost weight and her pain showed in the hollows of her face, the deep shadows beneath her eyes that had not been there before.

With a desperation born of despair she had tried to put him out of her mind. She had been prepared for scepticism when she had told him the truth about Eden, but the violence of his reaction had shaken her to the core. There was no way he would ever trust her. And if that hadn't been enough, his obvious shock when she'd

mentioned marriage, his later words, had told her that
marriage had been the last thing on his mind. What a
fool—what a gullible fool she had been!

So she had done her best to cling on to reason, get
the whole thing in perspective—immersing herself in her
work, accepting every invitation going, even contacting
old friends she hadn't seen in years. But nothing had
worked. The pain of loss was constantly with her, the
demoralising pain of fear—fear of the future, the empty
years of wanting him, loving him. She couldn't hate him;
it would be better if she could.

Dragging herself through to her sitting-room, she
picked up the phone and dialled Manda's number,
making her excuses, and Manda, concern in her voice,
told her, 'Have an early night, sweetie. Hot milk spiced
with Scotch is the best remedy I know of to ward off a
chill. Pity you couldn't make the shindig, though. Ty
Cary, the photographer, will be there—you remember,
we met him after the theatre last Friday? I've worked
with him since and he's smitten—dying to meet you
again. Still, there'll always be another time.'

Another time. The model's parting words echoed hol-
lowly inside her head. There would never be another
time, not for her. She had only ever truly loved once.
Waldo. Warts and all. Nothing he did and nothing he
said would make her stop loving him. That was the
tragedy of it all.

She could even understand the way he'd felt when
she'd attempted to explain about Eden. Waldo had loved
his foster brother, been proud of his literary success. And
he had believed those lies Lottie had passed on to him.
Why shouldn't he? He had no reason on this earth to
doubt them. Every reason to doubt her, Hannah.

She paced the confines of the room restlessly. Waldo had hated her for blackening Eden's character. And she, in her attempts to tell him the truth, had alienated him finally and irrevocably.

He had desired her as she desired him, had overcome his scruples and had been willing to go on from there, putting her past, as he saw it, behind them. But he had never loved her, never claimed to. Had he loved her, he would have believed her, would have asked her to be his wife, not his mistress.

Rubbing her hair dry, she wished she'd brought work home with her as she had done on the evenings during the last three weeks when she hadn't been going out. But on leaving work she had still—although unenthusiastically—been prepared to go to the party. There was no question, even, of staying home in case he should drop by or phone. He wanted nothing more to do with her.

On the Monday after he'd walked out on her he had, according to what Gerald had said, phoned the agency and asked for Roger Orme, requesting him to post Eden's unfinished manuscript to his London flat. That, Hannah felt, said it all. No way was he prepared to have any contact with her whatsoever. A promiscuous past was something his desire for her had led him to come to terms with. The truth about Eden had killed whatever feelings he'd had for her stone dead.

Her hair roughly dried and framing her pale face with vital abandon, she tossed the towel aside and poured herself a Scotch, drawing the curtains against the wet spring twilight, flicking on a single dim table lamp. Manda's suggestion that she had an early night held no charm. The hours of night were long enough and her fitful sleep too dream-haunted to make her want to prolong them in any way.

She wished she'd never met him. She would never have known the demands of love, the pain. Her life would have continued along the well-oiled tracks she'd laid, consciously and rationally, before love had robbed her of reason. Her love for him had been doomed from the start, a useless, pointless thing. Her soul had silently cried out to his, reached for him. But they had been unable to communicate except on a physical level. No matter how she'd tried she had been unable to get through to him.

Eventually, of course, he would learn the truth from Lottie. Lottie had said she would put things straight when next she saw him, and she had meant it. But it didn't signify. She had needed his trust, some sign that he believed in her—on her say-so, not that of someone else.

She tossed the remainder of her whisky back and poured another, her movements angry, almost vicious. Tonight she felt like getting well and truly drunk! She rarely drank, a Scotch or a couple of glasses of wine on social occasions, but tonight—what the hell! She had been branded by an expert, hadn't she? So she tossed the second dose down, too, amazed by the odd result, the sudden heat in her face, the light-headedness, the unnerving inclination to giggle at nothing.

It had been a long time since she had giggled, or even smiled, meaning it. Unsteadily, she slopped more spirit into her glass, and took it up, closing one eye as she frowned at the large amount of amber liquid that had somehow got into her glass. If she drank all that she would be legless. But she might sleep, might forget the lean dark devil who haunted her day and night. And she would wake with a monumental hangover, the tired little voice of reason reminded.

But the voice of reason was little, and tired, so it wasn't difficult to ignore it, and the glass was at her lips when the doorbell rang, sharply imperative.

Dear ole Manda, she decided tipsily, come to see how she was, to show off her party finery, perhaps—she'd said she'd bought something sensational for the occasion because she had the suspicion that James was about to propose, and she about to accept, if he did. And she was aiming to make sure he did!

Hannah put the glass on the drinks tray, then, her bare feet weaving a little, she wobbled to the door, aware of the vacuous smile on her face—whisky-induced. One thing was sure, she told herself tartly, the Scotch in the glass was going back in the bottle, or down the sink. Drinking was a fool's way round any problem.

It seemed to take hours of fumbling to get the door open and she got crosser with herself by the second. And when she finally dragged it open and saw Waldo there she knew she most definitely was going to sign the pledge!

DTs now, she groaned inwardly, her liquor-hazed brain neatly conjuring up the one person in the world who would have crossed to the other side of the world if he saw her coming!

'Hannah?'

She opened her eyes again and he was still there, filling the door frame, and her eyes drank in every feature, lovingly, longingly, pain still there but buried beneath the joy of seeing him. It would surface again, the pain, she knew that, stronger than ever. Already, as she stepped aside allowing him to brush past her, it was impinging cruelly. She had never thought to see him again, cer-

tainly not here, and it assuredly did not matter that she
was looking an unholy mess, the old terry robe belted
loosely over her nakedness, her face pale and strained,
her hair a wild, tangled mane. Because whatever he had
come for it wasn't his intention to stand and admire, to
toss compliments in the air.

He was wearing a thin black sweater and narrow-fitting
dark trousers, and his tanned skin was drawn tightly over
hard, high cheekbones, his mouth compressed to a long,
suffering line.

He looked entirely menacing, his glittering black eyes
holding an emotion she couldn't read but which sobered
her all the same. Gone was the spurious, alcohol-induced
euphoria, fear and grief and loss taking its place, and
she passed the tip of her tongue over trembling lips.

'Why are you here?'

'To apologise.' The unlikely words took the breath
from her body and as she groped feebly to understand
them he swung round to face her, his eyes probing hers,
drifting down, touching her body, and by the time they
came back to lock with hers again she felt as if every
inch of her flesh had felt the caress of his hands.

'I hope you'll forgive me, Hannah.' The tone pleaded
yet rang with confidence, which was a peculiar amalgam,
she decided fuzzily, visibly sagging at the knees when he
added, 'Marry me,' the soft command brooking no
refusal.

Blindly, her hands reached out to find the support of
the back of a chair, but found his hands instead. Gentle,
yet totally in command of the situation, those hands
pulled her quivering body close to the hard length of
him, his arms going round her as he found her parted

lips with his, expertly opening them to his demands, probing, controlling, branding her.

She clung to him, to the dream, her fingers tangling in the crisp darkness of his hair, a moan of need torn from her as he eased her robe from her burning body, strong hands, hands that carried overt seduction in their every sensitive feathering movement, moulding her from shoulder to thigh, leaving no inch of flesh untouched, alive with a thousand yearning pinpricks of desire. Then, his mouth still locked with hers, he lifted her effortlessly in his arms, slowly carrying her to the bedroom, and she felt reality receding, place and time blurred, out of focus, their bonding the only reality that was.

He lowered her to the bed and she felt the cool softness of the patchwork spread against the heated silk of her skin, the fire of his lips as he bent to kiss her breasts, his hands cupping each as he tormented rosy nipples with his tongue. And then, when she thought she could bear the ecstasy no more, he proved to her that there was more to come. Much more as hands and lips moved over the flat planes of her belly, parting her thighs.

She was breathing harshly now, the rasping rhythm matched to his, and, without her being conscious of how he'd done it, he had removed his own clothing and skin was welded to skin, creating fierce havoc. There was no turning back now; the urgency of his body told her that. They had come so far along this road—— Not that she wanted to turn back, did she? She loved him.

Moving her head languorously, she met his dark passion-glazed eyes, felt the demand, the hot urgency, heard his smoky voice, thickened with need as he buried his head in the cleft between her breasts. 'God, how I want you, Hannah!'

'Want' but not 'love'. The demon that was cold reason staked a tiny claim on her love-drowned mind. He had wanted her before, but had walked out, hating her. Now he was back. Had apologised, offered marriage. So what had changed? Lottie—*of course!*

Hannah was stone-cold sober now, seeing things as they were and not as she wanted them to be. Her hands stilled against the smooth warm skin of his back, mindlessly registering the strong play of muscles. He had seen Lottie and she had told him the truth. And he had believed her, he'd had to, and had come back to her, free to acknowledge his physical need of her again, throwing the offer of marriage in because he had a conscience.

It wasn't good enough.

Desire drained from her body, leaving it limpid, hopeless. He had never once believed in the basic integrity of Hannah Sloane, only in what others had said of her, the way others had viewed her. Now, he had to believe the truth of what had happened between her and Eden, because Lottie had spelled it out. But it could never be enough. She had some pride, even where he was concerned; she needed to be regarded on her own terms, not as a nebulous creature, given shape and form only by the thoughts of others, to him more credible, witnesses.

For their relationship to have been anything other than a hollow sham she had needed him to believe in her of his own will, using his own intelligence, his own judgement. He hadn't, and now it was too late, too late to go back. He had at last believed the truth, not because she had said it was so, but because Lottie had.

'When did you see Lottie?' She pushed the words past the dryness of her throat and his lips left the suckling enjoyment of her breasts, finding the delicate skin beneath one ear.

'Sssh,' he bade her huskily. 'We've wasted so much time. Don't talk. Love me.' And when she jerked her head away he raised himself on his elbows, his eyes puzzled, lost. 'Just love me. Let me love you.'

She would always love him, but not in the way he meant right now. 'No.' Somehow, she found the strength to deny him, to roll from beneath him, but when she would have left the bed his arms held her, gently, his voice soothing.

'What is it, sweetheart? Tell me.' The sensuous touch of his fingertips, moving over her face, was difficult to ignore. Her body wanted to respond, to do anything he asked of her, be everything he asked of her. But it could never be perfect, as love should be, not now.

'Tell me,' he repeated, and she stared blindly at the ceiling, repeating her question.

'When did you see Lottie?'

'What kind of a question is that—at a time like this?' His tone was grim, but flicking him a wide glance she saw softness in his eyes.

'When?' she repeated stonily.

'I really don't recall.' The wealth of forced patience almost made her smile. But she was beyond smiling now, at anything, and she doggedly tried again.

'Some time during the past three weeks, wasn't it?'

'Hell, no!' As if he sensed her deadly seriousness, he levered himself up on one elbow, his black eyes intent on the smooth purity of the profile she presented to him. 'I don't know what this catechism is all about, sweetheart, but if you need to know how Lottie is then I can tell you she sounded fine when I spoke to her and David on the phone last week.'

'Did she have anything—important—to tell you?' She didn't look at him, she couldn't, and he sighed, a smile in the sound.

'Only that the daffodils are better than ever this year.'

Her heart leapt then, sending the blood thudding through her veins with an upsurge of hope. She had felt that Lottie wouldn't discuss Eden on the phone, certainly not if she and David were sharing the call. But she'd had to be sure.

'Then you haven't actually seen her?' she questioned quickly, hope hanging on a thread.

'No. I spent the last three weeks at Eyesore, but I didn't visit my foster parents. I didn't have time. I spent every daylight hour tramping the marshes thinking of you. Every hour of darkness lying awake, thinking of you— and of what you'd tried to tell me.'

He sat up, the skin of his back looking like oiled silk in the deepening twilight that seeped into the room, and Hannah expelled the breath she hadn't known she was holding as he told her roughly,

'I was in a mess. Dammit, woman, you'd got under my skin and I couldn't rid myself of you, the touch of you, the thought of you, the scent of you. You'd blinded me to everything else. But I'd believed what Lottie had told me and I'd built on that—Gerald Orme, Edward Sage, who knows how many others—the way you'd responded to me at the cottage, even though I'd lost you a holiday and maybe even given you a few grey hairs from fright at the way I'd hijacked you,' he clipped. 'But there, on my own, I started to use my brain at last. I couldn't reconcile what I thought I knew of you to the way you made me feel—protective, a mass of needs. And you stayed to look after me when you could so easily have walked out—that wasn't the act of a self-seeking bitch. Even so, when I actually began to suspect that I might be falling in love with you—the day we left—I had to dredge up Eden's phantom and put it between us, to get the strength of will to make myself believe that all there was between us was old-fashioned lust. And then, at the cottage, I read Eden's manuscript and it was rubbish, and I knew then that it hadn't started out as something good, unfinished because he'd been tormented by his love for a heartless bitch. And somewhere along the line,' he turned to her then, his eyes haunted, 'I knew you bore about as much resemblance to the picture of you I'd made in my mind as a lump of mud does to a star. I believed your truth. You'd once spoken about the various shades of the truth, and I believed yours. I love you, it's that simple, and if you'll forgive me for the things I've done and said, if you'll marry me, I'll spend the rest of my life atoning.'

It was too much, too sweet, and tears choked her as she held out her arms to him. He entered the loving haven of them, his voice thick as he told her, 'I love you, Hannah. Love you. Say you'll forgive me, love me, too?'

She said it, her body echoing the vow silently, but with devastating effect, and later, much later, she informed him lazily,

'I do like the way you atone. But I think I've some atoning of my own to do now.'

'How so, woman?' He pulled her effortlessly on top of him, long, steel muscled legs imprisoning her body against his, pelvis to pelvis.

'I spent most of my time thinking you were an un-believable boor, a sadistic bastard, in fact,' the willing prisoner stated demurely, wriggling her hips a little in a way that wasn't demure in the least, her storm-green eyes widening in rapturous surprise as she felt the mounting hardness of him, even though she had teasingly insti-gated it.

'So we're quits,' she reminded him with husky diffi-culty. 'We meet as equals.'

It was nearly dawn when she woke and found him watching her and she mumbled blearily, 'Don't you ever sleep?'

'Not when I can look at you, no.'

'Then you'll be a wreck before you're forty,' she grinned sleepily, loving him more than life, stretching, unashamed in her nakedness, her senses leaping to life as she saw the devouring passion in his eyes.

'And that I won't regret,' he said thickly. 'But if I'm going to keep up sufficient strength to enable me to stay in bed all day—with you—I'm going to need a coffee. Strong and hot. Get to it, woman!'

Grinning, Hannah rolled off the bed, padding to the kitchen, revelling in her nakedness, the entirely satis-factory sensations of utter wantonness. She carried a tray through, perching on the edge of the bed as they drank their coffee, her happiness not easily contained, bub-bling through in her voice as she told him, 'I'm going to be late for work. You can catch up on your rest while I'm out earning a crust,' but he disabused her in no un-certain terms.

'The hell I will. You'll phone your resignation. We're going to be married as soon as I can arrange it, and we'll be moving to Moorgate as soon as the restorers are out. And I want a full-time wife.'

'You didn't want a full-time mistress,' she reminded him lazily and he shook his head, sobering suddenly. 'I wouldn't have had the right. I hadn't admitted then, even to myself, that I loved you. Loving you gives me rights. The right to tie you to me permanently. I knew I wanted you with me, though, but was too damned stupid to understand why. I thought it was lust, when all the time it was love. When I walked out on you I thought it was for ever. I'd never felt so devastated in my life.'

'But you went ahead with the purchase of Moorgate, even after——' The rest of the sentence was left delicately unsaid and he grinned lopsidedly.

'Yes, even after. I knew I had to live there, because of you. I'd seen how you immediately fell in love with the place. And even if I hadn't come to my senses I would have made my home there, a brooding old bachelor.'

'That I can just see!' Hannah taunted, then gasped with pleasure as his hands trailed the path his eyes had been blazing on her body.

'And what,' he questioned with mock severity, 'happened to Edward Sage?'

'I don't believe I'm hearing this!' She squirmed away from him, her body going rigid. How could he rake that murky ground now? Now, of all times! 'How did you find out I'd been seeing him, anyway?' she snapped. 'It was years ago.'

'I know. The long eyes of the vengeful, perhaps?' An eyebrow tilted wickedly and she growled, 'So tell me!'

'Easy.' He handed her his empty cup and she banged it down on the tray, her face hot and cross as he lolled back against the pillows, the lord of creation! He told her easily, 'I wanted to dig the dirt on the woman who'd betrayed my brother, and it wasn't difficult to trace your old landlady, via a certain talkative middle-aged lady who works for Roger Orme. And the landlady—a vicious-tongued baggage, if ever I met one,' he continued loftily, 'was only too happy to tell me how the prim vicar's daughter wasn't averse to having an affair with a married man.'

'Of all the——' Hannah bit back a word that would have been entirely out of place on the tongue of a vicar's daughter. 'If you must know,' she lobbed him a scathing glare, 'there never was an affair. He wouldn't have said no to one, because that was what he'd been after all along, but I, green as grass, asked him to wait until we were married—like a good little vicar's daughter!' Her tone, downright nasty now, raised an infuriating grin and she positively spat, 'When I gently imparted that little pearl of information he told me he was already married, thank you very much, and that was the last I saw of him. Are you,' she growled, 'trying to pick a quarrel, by any chance?'

'Only a very little one.' He reached for her, dragging her down beside him. 'And I can promise you that the making-up will definitely be out of all proportion.'

'Promise?' Hannah wasn't protesting, she was melting.

Then he said, 'I never, ever, go back on a promise. And while we seem to be in a talkative mood——' he drew her willing hands down the length of his body, effectively proving that conversation was not what he really had in mind '—maybe you'd like to tell me what all that "Lottie" business was about? Lottie this, Lottie that?'

'Mmm.' Hannah was too engrossed in what her hands were discovering, in what his hands were doing, in the delightful prospect of a blissful married life with this lean dark devil to bother about Lottie. 'Maybe. Later. Lottie will explain. One day.'

And that, as far as they were both concerned, was enough about that.

# Six exciting series for you every month... from Harlequin

### *Harlequin Romance*·
### The series that started it all

Tender, captivating and heartwarming...
love stories that sweep you off to faraway places
and delight you with the magic of love.

◆

### *Harlequin Presents*·
### Powerful contemporary love stories...as individual as the women who read them

The No. 1 romance series...
exciting love stories for you, the woman of today...
a rare blend of passion and dramatic realism.

◆

### *Harlequin Superromance*®
### It's more than romance...
### it's Harlequin Superromance

A sophisticated, contemporary romance-fiction
series, providing you with a longer,
more involving read...a richer mix of complex plots
realism and adventure.

# Harlequin American Romance™
## Harlequin celebrates the American woman...

...by offering you romance stories written about American women, by American women for American women. This series offers you contemporary romances uniquely North American in flavor and appeal.

◆

# Harlequin Temptation™
## Passionate stories for today's woman

An exciting series of sensual, mature stories of love...dilemmas, choices, resolutions... all contemporary issues dealt with in a true-to-life fashion by some of your favorite authors.

◆

# Harlequin Intrigue™
## Because romance can be quite an adventure

Harlequin Intrigue, an innovative series that blends the romance you expect... with the unexpected. Each story has an added element of intrigue that provides a new twist to the Harlequin tradition of romance excellence.

# Harlequin Books

PROD-A-2